Publisher's Note:

Thank you for purchasing this book. It began as an idea, was shaped by the creativity of its talented author, and was subsequently molded into the book you have before you by a team of editors and designers.

Like all EDGE books, this book is the result of the creative talents of a dedicated team of individuals who all believe that books (whether in print or pixels) have the magical ability to take you on an adventure to new and wondrous places powered by the author's imagination.

As EDGE's publisher, I hope that you enjoy this book. It is a part of our ongoing quest to discover talented authors and to make their creative writing available to you.

We also hope that you will share your discovery and enjoyment of this novel on social media through Facebook, Twitter, Goodreads, Pinterest, etc., and by posting your opinions and/or reviews on Amazon and other review sites and blogs. By doing so, others will be able to share your discovery and passion for this book.

Brian Hades, publisher

THE
PATCH PROJECT
BRITTNI BRINN

EDGE SCIENCE FICTION AND FANTASY PUBLISHING
An Imprint of HADES PUBLICATIONS, INC.
CALGARY

The Patch Project

Copyright © 2018 by Brittni Brinn

This is a work of fiction. Names, characters, places, and incidents are the products of the author's imagination or are used fictitiously and are not to be construed as real. Any resemblance to actual events, locales, organizations, or persons, living or dead, is entirely coincidental.

EDGE SCIENCE FICTION AND FANTASY PUBLISHING
An Imprint of HADES PUBLICATIONS, INC.
P.O. Box 1714, Calgary, Alberta, T2P 2L7, Canada

The EDGE Team:
Producer: Brian Hades
Acquisitions Editor: Michelle Heumann
Edited by: Heather Manuel
Cover Design: Peter Brinn
Book Design: Mark Steele
Publicist: Janice Shoults

ISBN: 978-1-77053-172-7

All rights reserved. No part of this book may be reproduced, scanned, or distributed in any printed or electronic form without written permission. Please do not participate in or encourage piracy of copyrighted materials in violation of the author's rights. Purchase only authorized editions.

EDGE Science Fiction and Fantasy Publishing and Hades Publications, Inc. acknowledges the ongoing support of the Alberta Foundation for the Arts and the Canada Council for the Arts for our publishing programme.

Library and Archives Canada Cataloguing in Publication
CIP Data on file with the National Library of Canada
ISBN: 978-1-77053-172-7
(e-Book ISBN: 978-1-77053-171-0)

FIRST EDITION
(20180226)
Printed in USA
www.edgewebsite.com

Acknowledgements

Michelle Heumann — for keeping these characters alive. From the very first chapter, you encouraged me to keep writing. Thank you so much for believing in this book.

Miller Square Starbucks — for supporting my coffee addiction and my creative projects. Sorry for naming a character after you.

The Supina family — your home is a hub for artists and dreamers, and I cannot thank you enough for your wisdom, encouragement, and midnight discussions.

The Green Bean Café — where community happens, where artists and musicians sling coffee and ideas, where I write and edit and feel at home.

Hanan Hazime, Shawna Diane Partridge, Cindy Chen, Lydia Friesen, Amilcar John Nogueira, Joe LaBine, Jasper Appler, Janine Marley, Joey Ouellette — you writers, you inspirations, you voices of reason, you imaginative dreamers, you poets on the fringe.

All of my writing teachers — Mrs. Lake, Lisa Martin-DeMoor, Jasmina Odor, Karl Jirgens, and Susan Holbrook.

Heather Manuel, Brian Hades, and everyone at EDGE who made this book better.

To my family — Chelsea, Maxine, Murray, Andy, Jean, Arwen, Tye, my grandparents, my aunts and uncles, cousins — our lives are woven in unfathomable patterns; you are all a part of mine.

Dedication

For Peter. Punk and poet and healing post-apocalypse. I love you.

BOOK ONE

Chapter One

Candles

May was leaning against the kitchen sink, staring through the broken glass window. Her hands, still wrapped in strips of cloth, held a chipped porcelain mug to her chin as a faint whisper of mint wound its way around her face. As far as she could figure, they had enough tea to last a month, maybe two if they re-steeped the used tea bags. After that, they could mix the herbs into rice, use the filters for fuel. They had to keep everything now.

Isak stole in behind her, his arms warm around her midsection, his chin digging pleasantly into her shoulder. He saw what she did: a dull copper plain under a slate sky with nothing else for miles.

"Hey," he said, rubbing her pale cheek with his dusky one. "Know what today is?"

"The end," she replied, leaning away to sip at the weak tea. It loosened her throat, and she cleared it with a tense cough. Isak remained silent. She returned her attention to the dreary panorama that had once featured a fenced-off soccer field ringed with houses.

"Happy Christmas." He slipped something into the pocket of her cardigan as his arms vaporized into air. A couple seconds later she heard him appear in the living room with a gasp as his body settled into the back of the couch.

"I didn't think it mattered anymore," she said loudly enough, but he didn't reply. Placing the mug down on the counter, she reached up a bandaged hand to trace the hole in the glass. Through it, the sky was solid cloud, as if bolt after bolt of gauze had been draped over them; there had been no other sky, not for months. Not since that day.

The bleak silence of the outside crumpled her. She pulled her hand back to her tea, listening to a hum on the wind that wasn't there.

May and Isak lived in a house on what used to be Holly Street. There used to be many houses on the street, tall ones with white siding and red trim. Just like there used to be people, walking, on bicycles, pushing baby carriages, red, green, yellow, blue dabs of acrylic paint on the picture of suburbia. There was a red postbox on the corner covered in posters for music teachers and house cleaners. A fountain splashed brightly in the park at the center of the cul-de-sac, next to a purple and gold play structure with tire shards scattered around it, all recycled. Mr. and Mr. Otteron lived on their right, elderly Ms. Carol on the left. They had moved in last out of everyone, and were welcomed with cakes, bouquets, and house calls, the gifts of the already established. It had been a nice community, the closest thing you could get to country neighbors in the city. Young May and Isak, managing a mortgage and waiting for the kids to come, spending their slow evenings in the apple-tinged air—

May broke away from the window, sharply turning toward the stopped clock over the plastic dining table. Slightly off center, a half-used candle melted into a porcelain saucer edged in gold. She began fidgeting with the linen tablecloth, tugging it to the left, pulling the candle to line up with the downward pointing hands.

"Isak, how many candles do we have left?"

"About three," he answered. She heard him shift on the cracked leather couch. Doubtless his legs were giving him trouble again. Not only were the candles running low, but so were the matches, the tea bags, the cans of soup, the sheets she had been ripping up to use as bandages. The blood seeping from the gouges in Isak's legs had scabbed over before breaking open again in a steady excrement of blood-tinged pus. It was impossible to wash the sick yellow stains out of the material, especially since she was running low on vinegar.

She felt the heat of his arms in a band around her, but it was only a memory. He had put something in her pocket. May pulled out a chair from the kitchen table, taking out a small velvet box. Wiping a hand over her face, she slowly set herself in the cool plastic seat and rubbed the soft lid with her thumb. She sat and wondered, thinking of Isak's earthy eyes and the wounds in his legs.

The hinge on the box was tight and snapped the lid shut against her tired, one-handed attempt to push it open. She tried again, prying until lid and base sat at ninety degrees in front of her. The item inside shone against the deep blue cloth; it could've been a star if stars were cube shaped.

"Isak," she breathed, smiling at the tiny block of sugar.

"Like it?" he asked from the living room. "I had it ordered special."

May poured half of what was left of her tea into another mug, augmenting the volume of each with what was left from the kettle. She took the sugar cube, scratching off the tiniest amount into the steaming hot water. It smelled wonderful. Taking down a brightly painted tray from on top of the empty refrigerator, May glanced over toward the window. The day was dimming, the land becoming one with the empty sky. The tone of the kitchen was graying too, and May balked, hurrying, taking the unlit candle and closing the sliding wooden door behind her.

Colors in the living room were still distinguishable, the Impressionist-style painting hanging corner to the bay window quietly singing of light. She came around to the front of the couch, setting the tray on the floor and fishing in her pocket for a match.

"I knew we were running out," Isak said about the sugar, reaching out and guiding her down beside him. "We don't need to light it now."

May handed Isak a mug. "Thanks. Really sweet of you."

They both smiled. "I thought you'd notice one was missing, but you never said anything."

She had kept the sugar bowl behind the toaster, so as not to tempt them with the last jigsaw of refined sweetness left in the house. But like all things, that too had ended. The bowl, now set under the kitchen clock, held one lone cube with a corner rubbed off.

May sensed Isak's body stiffen. He was singing an old carol, his eyes fixed on their ghost-like reflections in the dim bay window. *"The holly and the ivy when they are both full grown, of all the trees that are in the woods..."*

May rubbed Isak's thigh soothingly. Isak squinted his eyes and continued singing, gripping the arm of the couch and turning his face toward her. She opened her mouth to join him, singing in her small, wavering voice: *"O, the rising of the sun, and the running of the deer..."*

"Embrace me?" he pleaded, and she leaned in toward him, smelling tea on his ragged breath and feeling his heart pounding the inside of his chest. "I'm not going anywhere... Don't worry, May... I want to... I want to stay here with you." He gasped, moaning, "It hurts..."

"I'll get some water."

"Don't... If you leave, I'll skip ahead to when you're with me again..."

She would be quick. She would get the basin and the water out of the kitchen, tuck the newly folded cloths under her arm, and talk the whole way. Engage him.

"Guess what my favorite Christmas carol is?" she queried, winking.

A weak grin appeared on Isak's strained face. "'O Holy Night?'"

"Nope. Guess again," she said, pushing herself off the couch and opening the door into the kitchen. "Come on Isak, you know me, and this one's easy."

His voice was steadier. "'Joy to the World?'"

A scoffing laugh escaped her as she poured water from an ice cream pail in the sink into a silver bowl. A cloth bag with a green recycling symbol on the side hung from a hook by the door, leading into what used to be their backyard. May snatched it down and hitched it over her shoulder.

"'Once in Royal David's City.'"

"I've never even heard of that one." She had everything she needed. Steadily, as to not splash the water over her bandaged hands, May re-entered the living room. "Do you want a hint?"

Isak's face was calm again, though he winced as she started to unwrap the soiled strips from around his left leg. "All right."

"It's in a minor key." Yellow-edged gashes glared up at her. His leg was festering and swollen and damp. Readied supplies from the reusable bag were poured out onto the floor. She squeezed a quick stream of anti-bacterial hand soap into the water, swirling it with a dish towel.

"Oh, that narrows it down considerably." Isak squinted. "'We Three Kings?'"

May pulled on a thick pair of blue rubber gloves and proceeded to wring out the cloth, the torrent of excess water creating a lovely distraction.

"I know what it is." He grinned. She spread the towel over his leg.

"Oh, do you really?"

"Most definitely."

May rubbed the red tip of a match against a piece of sandpaper. "Sing it for me." She held the flame to the wick, leaving the spent match on the gold-edged plate.

"It's just like a candlelight service," Isak said.

May looked up expectantly, but he had forgotten about the song. His face was touched by candlelight and shadow, dark eyes glossy and at peace. She worked a needle as long as her finger out of its cardboard envelope and held it in the flame. "Okay..." she sighed. "Don't skip out on me, all right?" She lifted the towel and punctured one of the puss-filled bubbles as Isak gripped his forearms and started to sing.

Chapter Two

Pinot Noir

The thick green glass bottle left her hand in an ambitious arc that ended in gleaming shards. An emerald firework, they exploded out from the point of contact, a stale brick wall drained and hanging like a corpse in the dull midnight. Pieces scattered along the sidewalk, smiling teeth of small creatures looking for feet to bite. Fatal if ingested, useful for impaling. Vibrant. Cruel. Beautiful. Pinot approved of her handiwork by stepping over it, her ragged Converse kissing the patches of concrete as seals. She wished for another bottle to hurl, and one appeared, hovering in front of her.

"Still thirsty?" moaned a voice from over her shoulder. The arm holding the bottle aloft pressed down across her collarbone. She reached, straining against the thick rope of arm, her hands closing over the glossy neck, trying to pull it free.

"Let me have it, Miller." Her eyes felt dry; she blinked harder to wash out the pain, to see the green outline more clearly. "Let go!"

Miller eased off, keeping his hand loosely on her shoulder as Pinot screwed off the cap, her fingers shaking. Her nails were blunt and cracked, and she wore a silver ring featuring a rose on her third finger. The foil around the top of the bottle was crisp and vocal; she pulled it free with her unsteady, dried-out fingers and tipped the mouth to her lips. The purplish liquid swirled in an emerald-tinged whirlpool, draining down into her full consumer mouth. She relented, swallowing.

"That's good juice," she sighed, and wiped her mouth on the inside of her wrist. Her tattoo of an infinity symbol was stained with wine dregs. Miller took his turn, twisting his head and looking as if he was about to bite the bottle neck clean in half. His dreads hung over his eyes, blond and blue, dribbles and splashes of bruise woven into his spun clumps of hair.

"*Aaaah,*" rushed out of his thin, drawn lips in a dissolution of fumes.

They staggered under the dim haze of midnight, passing forth and back the bottle of berry blood. The rigor mortis binding the buildings with boarded up windows and bleak brick skins gave way to older remains, sagging houses and skeletal warehouses. The road broke into pieces of gravel; the ditches became soggier with phosphorescent sludge foaming along the edges. Pinot tapped the last of the wine from the bottle, catching drops in her open mouth. "Empty!" she squealed, hurling the bottle through the glass front of a bus shelter. It exploded into sound, cubes and cracks of blue-green glass hailing onto the ground in a chorus of termination.

"Shaddup a second." Miller muffled her celebratory exclamations with a hand that smelled of rusted nails. A dull pounding hovered in the air, a chord of mechanical repetition mingled with fragments of indiscernible language. They both relaxed. "Thought it might be the Opaldine gang," he said, moving his hand from her mouth onto her shoulder. "Didn't think we were far out enough to run into Partiers." They sat against the empty back of the bus shelter, the bench an island in the puddle of glass. Miller scooped a handful of the shards and shifted them around his palm. He took out a thinly tubed flashlight and shone it through the pile. Refracted checkers shimmered on the tin roof, haloing around his dark silhouette. Pinot stared up with unfocused eyes. They had reached the edge of the city, beyond which was a rolled-out dough of land, sprouting hairs which grumbled gray in the slow wind.

The distant noise which had so startled Miller was growing in volume, the pounding filling up the empty front of the shelter, until it rolled past in an ongoing flow of dull bronze. They had eyes, these Partiers, no obvious legs, and domed bodies that moved deliberately forward. From an indistinguishable part of the land, they rose and sunk into the city like alligators into a swamp. They spoke a language which neither Pinot nor Miller had ever tried to understand. As a rule, the Partiers kept to themselves. They passed the busted bus shelter without recognition.

The 'scape was empty again. Pinot sucked the insides of her cheeks, leeching out the remnants. Her voice cracked as she turned her head to look at Miller. "Can't we have some more?"

"There isn't any," Miller explained, in a way that allowed for no argument. Even if he did have another bottle sloshing around in his backpack, Pinot knew better than to ask again. Kicking some loose glass with the steel toe of his combat boot, Miller leaned over and started chewing on her neck. She pushed his face away, propelling herself out of the shelter.

"Let's go somewhere first," she said, jumping erratically and pounding her feet into the ground. Miller rose slowly, following her out into the wilderness, a grimace etched from ear to metal-plated ear.

"Pinot," he growled as a warning, but she kept on, weaving ahead of him and giggling crazily. The juice was sloshing around in her head, washing strange bloody visions up on the shore of her skull.

"Miller?" she asked, hopping on top of a twisted clump of metal and turning back toward him. "Did you throw them out afterward? Did you throw them out?"

"No, Pinot," he said. "I didn't. They're still in there."

She ran ahead a little farther, staggering, falling, copper-colored dirt grinding under her fingernails. "It was a great party, Miller. The music was sick, I felt—" Her face puckered a little. "You shoulda thrown them out!"

"It was their place," he said, crouching down beside her. "I took what I could and got out." He readjusted a strap, hiking the backpack further up onto his shoulders.

"You could've gotten more juice," she whined. "Miller—"

He was suddenly standing over her, his stained hair haggard around his face. "You should thank me, you piece of shit. What did you do anyway? Nothing." He impassively struck her.

Blood ran and dripped from the corner of her mouth. Pinot glared up at him, her glazed eyes burning, unable to raise herself from her knees, her jeans grinding into the dirt. Her teeth were smeared red; they nearly glowed as she started, from the painful core of her repugnant body, to laugh. "Almost better than the real thing." She smeared the blood up her cheek and licked her finger.

Miller pulled her up by the neck and sucked her lips into his. Pinot hung limp in his arms.

Chapter Three

Five-Four

Ed had been in a phone booth when it happened. He didn't remember who he had been talking to, or why he had been using a pay phone instead of his Android, but he remembered the moment all the lights on Highway 2 blacked out. The line went dead in his hand and he experienced a biting pain chewing its way through his eyes, into his skull, out through the buds on his tongue. He came to the next morning, a starburst of vomit hardened on the glass door and the front of his shirt.

The convenience store was home after that. In retrospect, he shouldn't have shattered through the front door. It weakened his defense against wild animals and the elements, although admittedly there was neither in the weird new existence he found himself living in. A piece of road, like a section of disconnected toy train track, flanked by gas pumps; the glass and corrugated-siding store with bars over the windows; and the telephone booth that had saved his life. His BMW with fresh cream interior had been swept away in whatever had happened that night he had pulled over to make a phone call.

He remembered the day he had discovered his ability to manipulate electronic devices. He was sleeping off a headache, spread out newspapers underneath him and a blue canvas jacket with yellow reflective stripes held tight to his chin. A bright spot lingered on the edge of his consciousness. At first, he found it incredibly irritable. *Trying to sleep, here,* he thought. *Go pester a zombie or something.* The annoying spot did not heed his warning. Muttering threats in his mind, he followed it, half-asleep, to the cathode of a fluorescent bulb. His eyelids opened to the buzz of cold artificial light overhead.

That had sparked some enthusiasm. Lights, the CD demo machine, the laptop in the cabinet under the lottery ticket display, he could use all of them, charging the circuits and manipulating data boards with his mind. The virtual gaming experience he had been polishing in Vancouver would have taken him no time at all with this newly acquired skill set.

If you were looking for a story, Ed was your man. He had subplots brewing constantly, could draft a storyboard in a day. His female characters could be a little one-dimensional, but the company guys didn't mind too much. Ed's games were successful because they targeted a certain kind of player, told a certain kind of story. Usually it involved excessive blood splatters, interstellar politics, and cool goggles, rounded out by well-crafted dialogue and distinctive character designs. Ed was a pro. He was passionate about his work, and that's why, someday, he was really going to make it. He already had the car to prove it. Well, had it, past tense. *Past, Present, and Future walk into a bar...* Bars were something else he missed. Places dim, packed, swirling with life and unfinished sentences. He missed sitting in some corner with a cold beer, an out-of-the-way observer of humanity.

"You've got something that draws people," Karl had told him once. He was a bartender, late thirties, a stocky, dependable guy with a stubbed nose, someone who took his duty of care seriously; any night of the week he'd be checking in with the people leaning on the bar, exchanging high fives with the regulars. Ed used to be one, until he met Kay.

Katherine, Karl's girlfriend, had striking blue-green eyes and an equally striking personality. She came in often to sit at the bar and go out with Karl on his smoke breaks, crushing at least three hearts throughout the course of a night. "She can't help it." Karl shrugged, trying to stay easy. "She's just too beautiful." To which Kay would offer him a kiss, and there they were, all made up.

"So, Karl tells me you're a writer."

It was a Saturday, and the bar was packed past fire safety limits. Ed pulled his focus away from a tight cluster of gents in suit jackets and jeans, who were undoubtedly from the university and thought themselves the intellectual backbone of the establishment. He turned his soft smile onto Kay, in all her bar-scene beauty. She stood next to him, leaning on the wall and sipping on a vodka cranberry. She too had been observing the young Voltaires and seemed amused.

"Well," Ed began in his charming, soothing, and innocent voice, "that's what they tell me."

She laughed just enough, her eyes sparkling. "And what do these people base their conjecture on?"

Wow, Ed thought to himself, *conjecture*. He smiled and shrugged to hide his delight. "Plot lines for video games, mostly. I've been known to do commercials from time to time."

"And how did you get into that area? Is it something you always wanted to do?"

Ed took the opportunity to lean in, and said, "I slept with the boss."

Kay glanced quickly over his expression and, seeing he was serious, merely shook her head. "If you really want it, that's what you have to do sometimes." It was said easily enough, but Ed noticed her rubbing her wrist. "What are you working on now?"

A real grin broke over his face and he moved up next to her so their shoulders were almost touching. "It's a great project. Are you a gamer? I mean do you play—? Never mind. I've, um, just submitted" — he took a swig of beer — "the preliminary work. I think it'll take."

"It must be exciting making your living like that. Doing something you love."

And that's when he moved in. It failed horribly and he spent the following three weeks in bed due to a minor concussion and a broken collarbone. Karl, seeing Ed's attempt, had cleared the bar, picked him up under the arms and thrown him bodily out into an alley. Ed had never been very athletic or muscular, and his artist's disposition didn't lend toward a quick recovery. He had to brood for a couple weeks first.

Ed stood up, shaking off the remembrances as he wandered over to the back wall of the store. *All right, baby,* he thought at the drink cooler. *Make me a happy man, will ya?* An hour later, he was sitting on the concrete stoop of the convenience store with an ice-cold bottle of cola in his hand. Not that the view was all that inspiring. It looked post-apocalyptic enough to backdrop nicely on some undead shooter game, or stand in for a desert op on some abandoned planet. Ed felt sad just looking at it. Bareness, grayness, emptiness. A blank stage and no one but himself to fill any of it.

Chapter Four

Paint Stick

The shovel was old, rusted, and heavy. It pressed down on May's shoulder, the bleached wooden handle chafing against her bare wrist. She was tired and the shovel was heavy and outside was unwelcome. She walked quickly across the unnaturally flat ground. Not a bump, not a depression, not a hair of grass or a monument of tree. It was a Badlands steamrolled, a Sahara sheet of new sandpaper. It was frightening.

Outside, the humming was louder, like a cluster of voices by an electrical generator or the faint buzz of the television from an upstairs room. If Isak had been able to handle the job she would never have left the muffling walls of their home. Maybe she could ask him to take over for her, skip forward a bit—

"No, no he can't, don't even think it," she told herself. "His leg would only get worse and you'd only be doing it because you're selfish."

She reached the row of paint sticks pounded down into soft piles of dirt. Each little grave was set about a meter apart. An open hole gaped to her left, secreting scents of excrement into the flat, dead air. She adverted her eyes upward and rolled up the loose gray sleeves of her knitted cardigan.

The rusted shovel head carved into the earth, pieces of rubbery topsoil, and then dry sand, flying from the new hole to the old. She descended past the stratified layers of copper, tan, and burnt-orange ringing the space that, once full, she would return to bury. Start over again.

May straightened herself from bending over the ready-to-use shit-hole and, using the shovel, packed the loose dirt over the previous one. She took the paint stick, stained green, from the back pocket of her jeans and marked another four days' worth of human waste. Back when they still had fresh food to eat, compost would join the natural matter to be buried, but that seemed like years ago.

Adrenaline coursed through her body. Her teeth ached. The ever-present hum surfaced between the pounding of blood in her ears, a clue waiting to be formed into a hypothesis. She could follow it, see where it led, accept what it was. The land lay flat as the undisturbed disc of water at the top of a rain barrel. If she ran off over it, she might fall in, and drown in the rush of land.

Hoisting the shovel and tipping a mock brim at the newly erected bump to civilization, May returned to the safe house as quickly as the uniform ground allowed, only to find that Isak was gone.

It had happened a few times before, following a disagreement or a particularly bad pain in his legs. Desire always proved itself too strong, even for as thoughtful a man as her husband. He had skipped forward; she hadn't known how far. Would it be like last time? Would it be days before she saw him again?

May folded up sheets, pushed the pull-out bed back into the couch, mopped up where Isak's spilled tea pooled on the laminated hardwood. She dusted the dead television, replaced an anthology on the ceiling-to-floor bookshelf. She perched on the edge of the couch, her hands in her lap, spinning two tired rings around and around her fourth finger. She let the back of the couch take her in, her eyes going vague over streaks of mid-afternoon light on the walls and the popcorn-textured ceiling.

Isak sighed beside her and eased his head back onto her thigh.

"Was I gone long this time?" he asked.

"A few hours."

He relaxed, studying the gray lines accenting the deep green and gold speckled walls. "I wondered what the afternoon sun would look like. That's all I wanted to see. That's all it took." His voice was lower than usual, dulled.

May looked down at his face. "What does skipping forward feel like?"

Isak didn't answer right away. His eyes searched hers, a line pressing between his eyebrows. "Nothing. It's like the unnoticeable darkness when you blink."

May tipped her head back to the ceiling, breathing deeply through her nose, counting how many times her eyelids flickered open and shut. Isak shifted, turned his head.

"I'm sorry, May."

She absent-mindedly rubbed a cylinder of his black hair between her finger and thumb.

"I was going to paint today," she said. "Something set in a forest."

Isak sat up, his legs limply pointing to the other end of the couch, a hand spread tight against his temple. "The thing is, I can never go back. I can never go back, May, even if I wanted to."

She reached out a hand without looking away from the yellow fire hydrant outside their front window. Isak's loose shirt was warm, the curve of his back against her palm solid for now. She could differentiate each rib with each of her bony fingers, as her hand rubbed up and down, up and down until the light spent itself, tumbling into gray and then settling into a pool of black.

Chapter Five

Nowhere Land

It was sometime after the last lamppost, when all the stunted grass had ceased and the empty landscape had grayed over into a corpse with blue and purple tones under the pall. Miller and Pinot lay out on their backs looking up into the meaningless sky, their camp for the night composed of a pack and two bodies. Miller was in his shirtsleeves, Pinot with her socks and boots tumbled together next to her. Staring up and unspeaking. They lay and lay and lay and lay until Pinot sat up with her head thrown back.

"Mill-er," she said in a singsong voice. Her head lolled to face him. "Miller!"

His body shifted onto its side and settled into the unmistakable posture of sleep. Deterred, Pinot took a tube of lipstick from one of her many pockets and snapped off the lid. She ran it over her lips until they were completely black, throwing the empty cartridge far off where it plummeted into the dirt. Her hands crawled up into the roots of her hair, which she knew were growing in brown and darkening down into the inky black mat that hadn't felt the cool rush of water in weeks. Strands of hair caught on the dry cracks in her palms as she pulled them away. It was so still. She suppressed the urge to cry out and listen for an echo.

She wondered, strangely, what things would've been like if she'd stayed in school like her parents had wanted. "You're intelligent," her mother had said often enough.

"I don't understand why you'd want all those smarts to go to waste." Pinot imagined what it would've been like, waking up every morning to sit through classes in rooms packed full of people she didn't know, trusting someone on the basis of their credentials, handing in papers, working late every night so she could maintain a 4.0 average. Falling asleep in the library over textbooks on subjects she wasn't interested in, taking tests, eating lunch while on the way to her next class, dressing right, sleeping enough, involved in her school community. The thought made her physically anxious. "If you had gone in for that, you would've been dead," she told herself and burst into laughter.

"What the hell" — Miller pushed himself up, pinching the bridge of his nose — "is so funny?"

"School would've actually killed me," she said, before breaking into hysterics. Her hands rasped against each other. The thought, *I'm all dried out,* absently passed through her mind.

Miller wore a neon green shirt pierced through with safety pins, some parts held together with patches of duct tape. The chained leather pants that used to get soft in the sun were now scuffed up and cracking. All the alcohol had run out of his face, leaving it soggy and pale.

"Where are we going today?" Pinot asked with a hint of a sneer.

"Keep west," he said, taking in a deep, suffering breath. His eyes were shot through with an exhausted red.

Pinot lengthened her back along the earth, crossing her arms over herself. "Go back to sleep. There's no rush to get nowhere, is there?"

— «» —

They had been three days in the wilderness and two days sober when Pinot noticed the rust in the air, and patterns in the gray sheet hanging over them, as if something was trying to push its way through from outside. "That's messed up," she said as an aside, slipping a platonic arm around Miller's waist.

"Who cares about that?" he said. "We've got company."

She glanced over her shoulder. A man dogged behind them, about thirty paces. "One of *them*? One of the Opaldines?" she asked in a whisper. "How long has he been following us?"

"I don't know. I just looked back and noticed." He pulled at a stray dread behind his ear nervously.

"If he's after blood, we can't keep walking and pretend he's not there." Pinot unbuttoned a pocket and drew out a switchblade. "Let's find out what he wants."

Pinot and Miller skipped preliminaries, rushing toward him with whoops, almost running him down before splitting off and circling him in an easy, Sunday-in-the-park stroll. The man didn't appear to be armed; he remained steady, a water skin strapped across his back over a loose black hoodie and a worn-out set of canvas pants, his arms loose at his sides. He had dark skin and graying eyebrows; his shoulder length hair was untouched by age but his eyes were haloed in wrinkles.

"Where you from, old man?"

"Very far," came his answer.

"Thought you'd get some supplies from us, pilgrim? That we'd take care of you in your old age? No, I'm thinking it'll be the other way around." Miller was enjoying himself. He switched abruptly to a casual tone of voice. "Have you been through Portage? Have you seen the dead city?"

The man turned his eyes onto Pinot. "I've been there." She shuddered at the distressed lines that appeared in his face, reminding her of weeping in gutters and silent calls for help that had gone unanswered.

"And have you heard of us?"

"I know you," replied the man, looking straight at Miller, the pain in his eyes deepening. "Your name is Cauldor. You ran away from home, I can see that. What were you looking for when you abandoned your mother? Even you believe all things must be righted in the end."

Struck, as if in his stomach, Miller doubled backward. "You're a mad fuck!" Miller shouted at him, not daring to look into his face. "Get away from me." Miller grabbed Pinot by the arm, pulling her behind him as he staggered away.

"Let go of me, I'll kill him. I'll run back and stab him in the heart, Miller!" Pinot struggled lustily, but Miller didn't let go until the man was far out of their sight.

Exhausted and without food, they dropped to their knees. Miller uncapped a hidden flask from his pack and started drinking.

Chapter Six

Storms

May was outside tapping water from the fire hydrant when it began to rain. Slate-colored clouds wrung themselves in the gusts from the east. Dust swirled, waves appeared in the land, and the soft pattering of drops came to a crescendo in a crashing of cymbals and drums.

"Isak!" she cried, standing in awe of the downpour and shutting her eyes. The far-off humming was drowned out, the lightning flashed red and green through her closed lids. "Isak!"

He was there beside her, transported forward. It must have been from joy and amazement at the sudden, and first, change of weather since the day they had found themselves alone. "It's beautiful! Wonderful!" She felt him pulling her by the hands. "I forgot what it was like!"

She opened her eyes and found them facing the house, the mahogany door yawning open. "Not yet. Come on Isak, don't you want to dance in the rain?" She saw his mouth form words, but heard no sound; the pelting rain thundered against the earth, drowning everything else out.

Once inside, Isak tipped a pail of wash water over her head and then another over himself.

"What—" she gasped as the water cleared off her face. "What are you doing? I washed dishes in there!"

Isak glared at her, his face dripping. He took a towel and patted her face, her arms, her bare legs dry. "We have no idea — don't you think there could be harmful chemicals still in the atmosphere? We could be burned or eaten away by acid rain! Don't you think at all?"

May's face went blank. He toweled himself off, haltingly moving through the living room and into the kitchen. She tilted her head, looking up through where the staircase used to be, the rectangular hole in the ceiling with an acrylic field of poppies at the apex. Outside, the torrent of rain slowed to a light tapping on the roof.

Isak held the white gauze curtain away from the backdoor window, watching the rain. May leaned her hip against the sink, shifting her gaze from him to her shattered kitchen window. Why had that one broken and not the others? Why Isak's legs and not hers? He was fishing down the front of his shirt, fumbling with a chain and then a pendant, which he raised to his lips and blessed.

"What does it mean, do you think?" May asked. "No rain for months and then a downpour?"

"It doesn't mean anything." Isak dropped the curtain and lowered himself into a chair. May stared at him, her eyes wide. She had expected comfort, expected him to consider how it might fit in, how things would continue on as long as they were alive, how things would get better.

She reached her hands to his, locking into his dark eyes. She found the flaw in his left iris, a sliver of bronze that cut down toward the nearly indistinguishable pupil. "I know I've not been ... as positive about everything as you have, and I know it's been making it easier for you to skip forward—"

He took in a short breath. "That time was an accident, don't blame yourself for something that's my fault."

"No. I was wrong to be like that. You're not to blame either. For anything."

Isak raised her hands to his cheeks. When he spoke, his eyes roved the room, resting on items they had collected and placed around the home they had found together. "Poetry of our day focused on the object." He picked up the sugar bowl lid and spun it slowly before his eyes. "The meaning that could be derived from it. I thought maybe that's why we were the ones to survive; that we, our house, our possessions, maybe our domestic ... ecosystem was somehow the reason everything else had fallen away. Our lives still had purpose, May. But now I'm starting to think that our existence is just a fluke. We're going to live as long as we can and then die with no one to move our bodies off the floor." He ran one of his palms up and down the top of his leg. As he held her hand against his face, he pierced her with his eyes, and she nearly cried, they were so full of questions.

He swallowed and continued: "Sometimes, when I blink through time, I think there are voices or a set of eyes and I think, could it be the presence of God? But who am I to see visions? Or maybe we only think we're alive. Maybe we are the ones who disappeared and everyone else is wondering what the hell happened to May and Isak's little house on Holly Street."

His cheeks felt warm, they were flushed, his breath becoming more labored as his grip dug into her hands. "Why are we the ones who are still here?"

"You need to lie down, Isak."

"Things can never be put right, not when we don't even know what we're going on and on for. None of it, May, none of it is even—" His lips closed abruptly. Letting go of her hand, Isak turned his head to retch a splattering of thick yellow stomach juice onto the floor. He stared at it, slowly straightening himself, wiping his chin with the back of his hand. "You aren't feeling sick, are you, May?"

"No." She shook her head. "I'm fine."

"It can't be from the rain then... There was nothing wrong with the rain..." He pushed back the chair, the silver discs on the bottom of the legs stuttering against the floor.

The kitchen knew silence again. Only May was left. He had wanted to leave. This time, she knew, he had wanted to leave. She threw a dishtowel over the sour patch Isak had left behind and sat in his chair, wondering.

Massive alleys of destruction whir through cities, cracking foundations and uprooting lampposts, while a man sleeps with his back against a dumpster. A bed holding a sleeping child is carried off by a funnel cloud and set right side up in a wheat field. Tornados touch down and rip a whole house apart, but somehow the shower survives.

Chapter Seven

Ed's Gamble

He could find out where the lines were, and how many, and which ones had receivers. If he ventured out into the world of telecommunications and found nothing, however, that would be almost worse than never knowing; it would be better to go on living in ignorance of his own sad existence in an empty universe.

Ed was draining himself daily, throwing all his thoughts onto the long rolls of receipt paper and delving deeper into himself than he had ever dared before. His job had surrounded him with noise and busyness, the rush of working tempered with the spoils of glory. If there wasn't a story to finish or a meeting to attend, there were parties, fast cars, and his observation posts at nightclubs and bars around the city. There had never been time with just Ed. He was getting his fill of it now. Yep, just him and his thoughts, with the occasional trashy magazine or pulp fiction from the rack behind the counter. He'd exhausted the supply twice over, and could only find distraction in his writing. He wrote about people he used to know, setting them on different planets or setting them up on crazy dates, imagining himself in any number of places he had never been and would now never see. Moscow. Berlin. Tokyo. Heck, even Hawaii. Was there anybody out there? Were there any more movie theatres or libraries or golf courses or fancy restaurants or hipster joints or anything? What did Ed amount to, if Ed was all that was left? And if ever an alien race landed on Earth and discovered his preserved writings, would they give any weight to them at all?

The phone under the counter was painted gray, with labels on the quick dial buttons typed out in square letters that had started to fade to brown around the edges. The receiver was sticky on the back, with pop or gum or something; one of the hundreds of tiny bottles of hand sanitizer came in handy at that point. Once he had swabbed off the receiver, Ed searched around for a phone jack, and found one stuffed behind an empty ice cream pail holding a heavy-duty plunger. The cord didn't quite reach back to the desk, so Ed pulled over a stool and sat with the phone on his lap. He held the receiver up to his ear and closed his eyes. His mind sieved through the earpiece, spun around the coiled cord and entered the green and gold circuitry board. Everything in front of him was lit, he was in it and above it at the same time, watching his progress and traveling through the fine wires and synapses as if he were seeing it through a microscopic camera being pushed through a blocked artery, but a whole hell of a lot faster. He reached the splitting point, pausing to try and sense which circuits were still grounded, the lights at the end of the tunnels. He reached dead ends, phones that rang and rang and rang with no one to answer, zipping back and forth across the country until he was certain he had exhausted the entire continent.

The next phone he tried was a handheld model, with an answering machine built in. He traveled the circuit and found his way to the incoming call alert system, sounding the bell. He could hear the things he triggered, could experience all the pixels, all the finer details of refrigerating coolant systems and musical tracks. But the thing he was most unprepared for was the sound of a voice answering after the second and a half ring.

"Hello, this is May speaking."

May, he thought, *that's a nice name.* No, not nice, lovely, maybe even beautiful. Trees in bloom and the smell of rain. He caught the tail end of a missed sentence, waited for her to speak again.

"Hello?"

She sounded young, and very tired.

"Hello?"

She was waiting for him to say something.

"Hello?"

He could juggle the mechanics of the call and still manage to say — he opened his mouth but no sound came out. Struggling to voice a word, he didn't notice that she had hung up until two minutes later, when he remembered that he didn't have a voice anymore.

Ed had always been a smooth talker. A sweet-faced con with a dozen stories up his sleeve. He maintained all throughout his career that the only reason people invited him to parties was to listen to him talk. He would talk, telling stories of trivial events in his life and the politics of big game corporations. He would talk, to some sexy eyes in a corner, or a group of slim young men with their tie pins and spiked hair. Employees' kids liked listening to him. Especially Hannah. Hannah had been asking him for stories at staff Christmas parties since she was five. *Would have been fourteen now*, he thought to himself. Hannah had been a pudgy kid, no doubt, but she was sincere and smart and had a gentle way about her, and she always had a goodnight hug for him before her parents took her away at midnight, half-asleep.

He tried to speak again, straining his throat, taking a deep breath and trying with all his might to hurl sound out of himself. At one point, he managed a faint whistling sound, but that only depressed him more. He had to call May back, but how would he be able to talk to her if he couldn't form anything resembling a word? If he had gone into the army, at least he might have picked up Morse code. Maybe if he did something simpler? Banging the counter or taking words from the Celtic track in the music console. Or spelling. It would be a lot of effort, but hey, they were in no rush, were they? The world had been sucked dry, and they only had empty landscapes to look on and old memories to avoid. Maybe May would find spelling a welcome distraction. He knew he would.

Chapter Eight

Unknown Caller

Isak was reading; he was on the search for truth again and that was a good sign. May dug through a drawer, shaking a can of tomato soup with her other hand. Did the poetry of William Blake or Emily Dickinson or Eliot or Milton or Poe tell him anything he didn't already know? Isn't that why he loved them, because they already inexplicably resonated with his own soul? The truth, May reasoned, wasn't defined by what you could explain, but by what you couldn't. If truth was a word, then the world was deaf. And if they were the only ones left, could they hope to hear anything at all?

The open can of tomato soup had a serrated edge where the lid had been ripped off by a manual can opener they had found on their move-in day, abandoned at the back of a drawer. They had also found a broom, the old kind with straw bristles, leaning in the corner by the backdoor. Little things had been left behind and absorbed into their lives even though they didn't know who had left them or why. May was good at finding uses for things. The DIY movement had carried her along through college, where she had recycled hangers, old clothes, and wrappers into pieces of art.

She emptied the can into a fondue bowl set over a lit candle. She swished water around the coated inside of the can and added it to the bowl. What could you use empty cans for? They used to be good for holding paintbrushes.

Or hanging together with old cutlery to make wind chimes. But now she had no ideas. A bare stack of them loomed on top of the fridge, like some aloof Warholian pyramid.

The portion of soup she was warming would provide enough for three days, interspersed with weak thrice-boiled tea and a piece of canned fruit. Their pantry was nearing panic levels; only a half of the original cans and boxes were stacked neatly on the bottom shelf. The floor was concrete, and served them well as a larder since it stayed cooler than anywhere else in the house. May set a steaming jar of soup down on the pantry floor and took the rest in a mug to Isak.

A sharp bell interrupted their tranquil supper. May and Isak looked at each other in alarm and then toward the rounded mahogany table set flush to the side of the entryway closet.

"Should we answer it?"

May shrugged. "Where's the power coming from? That's what I want to know."

"Are we dreaming? Did I skip forward?"

Humming had entered May's sanctuary. She walked across the earth-patterned rug, stepped onto the hardwood, and lifted the black and silver cordless out of its dock. The screen display flashed green with UNKNOWN CALLER scrolling across in pixilated letters. "Hope it's not a telemarketer," she said wryly. She tapped the TALK button and held the dusty receiver up to her ear. "Hello, this is May speaking." It was a sweet, old, habitual way to answer the phone and, saying it, May could almost believe that she was back in the old house that still had solid stairs and a sense of hope in it.

The line was silent. May's eyes ran to Isak, bewildered; he was sitting on the floor surrounded by open books, the mug of soup at his lips.

"Hello, can you hear me? This is May. My husband and I are alive, are you there?"

She thought she could hear breathing, or maybe it was just static breaking up the empty connection. She waited. She waited a long time for any sign, but after a few more hellos, Isak stood up and vanished. She returned the phone to its stand. The red light on the side of the receiver indicating LOW POWER shone for a moment and then faded out. It was silent in the house once more.

Isak reappeared next to her, slipping an arm around her waist. "Anything?"

She shook her head thoughtfully. "I think someone was there."

"Maybe they'll call back. If it was anybody at all, they'll call back."

They set up a game of chess. May started on the defensive, her attention divided between the carved pieces on the board and the telephone. They played three games, Isak winning the last one. The captured players stood lined up against the edge of the board, like spirits of the fallen watching the outcome from the border, which, uncrossable, separated them from the land of the living.

"I've been reading *Frankenstein*," May said. "You know the part where the monster finds the cabin and watches the family inside through a crack in the wall? I feel like that family, or how they would've felt if they knew." She had cornered the king. "Who do you think it could've been?"

Isak sighed and placed a handful of royalty into a paisley green bag. The pieces, noble and rabble, clacked against each other as he pulled the drawstring tight, securing against escape attempts. "I don't know." He rubbed the back of his ear, his eyes unfocused. "Somehow there was enough power."

May pushed herself off the floor and over to the television. "Do you think...?" She pressed POWER; the screen remained a dull gray void.

"It could've been an influx from the power station, maybe one last effort at a full restart."

"That would still mean someone had to reboot it, and that there's still a functional power center somewhere out there. Either way, Isak, I don't think we're the only ones left. There has to be somebody else. Maybe even a doctor."

May went over to the phone, dialing old series of digits, but there were no answers, no dial tone. She set the receiver down and sighed. "Maybe they'll call back."

— ⟨⟩ —

The next day, May held the phone in her hand, looking out the front window; there wasn't much to see apart from the fire hydrant and the reflection of herself ghosting in front of the wasteland. Where their lawn had been was a stretch of dust with a few dried out strands of grass lifting feebly around the hydrant. A white wire fence marked out where their plum tree used to stand. They had chopped it down with an ax and burned it under pots and pans of dinners and mish-mashed breakfasts of oatmeal and pancakes and seared olives poured out from glass jars.

Suddenly, the same jarring ring hit May's brain in a heightened collection of hums. "Hello, this is May speaking," she answered, met again with the same fuzzy silence. "There's a fire hydrant outside of our window," she told maybe no one. "It's yellow with blue caps on the top and two sides. Our house is the only one in the middle of an empty plain that spreads out everywhere. It's a nice house. My husband's legs were injured when the stairs collapsed. He's ... out at the moment. Are you there?"

She was about to hang up when three beeps, someone pressing a key on the other end, evoked from her a cry of joy. "You are! Oh, God! You're somebody! And you're there."

Again, three even beeps, more delightful than a whole album of Nickel Creek's bluegrass symphonies.

"Talk to me, can you talk to me?"

One beep, signaling a negative.

"Oh... Is there anybody there with you?"

One.

"Do you have enough supplies?"

Three. Yes.

"That's good." There was a break as May struggled to find something else to say. "I'm sorry, I'm not very good with the phone. So ... can you call anyone you want?"

Yes.

"Have you talked to anyone else?"

No.

"Do you think ... we're the only ones left?"

A slight pause and then two short beeps.

"Maybe." May rubbed her forehead, trying to smooth out the increased volume of the ever-present hum. Was it because the phone was working? "I can't talk very long... I have this headache. You're not a doctor, are you? We could use a good doctor."

No.

"That's all right. What do you do, or did? Or... Well, I guess this is kind of limiting. But we'll figure something out. You could call back tomorrow. If you're not busy."

Yes.

"You can meet Isak too. If he's here."

Three.

"Goodbye. And, thanks for — thanks for calling."

A long tone. Goodbye, it said. Parting is such sweet sorrow.

Isak didn't reappear until May lay alone on the pull-out bed, staring up at the dark ceiling. She lay a hand on his chest and whispered, "They called back."

—— 《》 ——

The next afternoon, May and Isak sat together with the phone between them.

"I wonder how they found us."

"Phone book?" she ventured, twisting a strip of tea filter and dipping it into a lid full of white craft glue. When it hardened, it would burn down for ten minutes, secured in a reformed tube of melted wax.

The phone rang. Isak motioned with a tired hand and intent gaze, his wasted cheeks and weak brow framing his hunger-enlarged eyes.

"Hello, this is May."

A long beep. Greeting and farewell, the "aloha" of invented Morse code.

"How are you?" she asked, answered by three short beeps. "You're well?"

Three beeps again.

"Ask them about themselves," Isak prompted.

"Are you ... old?"

One.

She shook her head to Isak. "Younger. A teenager?"

No.

"Older?"

Three, yes.

"Are you in your twenties?"

Yes.

"Twenty-three?"

No.

"Older?"

Yes.

"Twenty ... seven? Oh, good guess."

Isak smiled, his wide, spiritual eyes creasing at the corners. May smiled in return.

"Are you ... male?" she asked, nodding to Isak when the beeps confirmed her question. "Are you..." She stopped herself. He had already said he was alone.

"Let me talk to him."

May entwined her fingers through his. "Here, I'm going to put Isak on the phone," she told the unknown caller, determined to find a way to learn his name by the end of the call.

Isak made the receiver look cumbersome between his spider fingers, the silver Medi-Alert bracelet he always wore resting on his arm almost down to his elbow. He didn't say anything and there seemed to be nothing to listen to. No beeps. Finally, he opened his mouth and said, "Hello." He passed the phone back to her, humming something.

"What is your name?" she asked the man on the other side of the unknown distance between them. "Can you spell it out somehow?"

After a pause, a string of beeps followed by a break and then another string came through.

"Sorry, can I hear that again?" She counted out five beeps to Isak, and then four.

"Ed," Isak said, turning himself toward the arm of the couch.

"Ed."

Yes.

May felt the watery heat of tears rise to her eyes. "Ed. It is so good to meet you."

─── ⟪⟫ ───

He called every day. Ed and May spelled back and forth, and although it was a long and involved process, May was glad of the series of beeps that she deciphered using a chart she had jotted down on the back of a gutted dictionary. She heard how he lived off of the bounteous junk food stocked shelf upon shelf in the convenience store that was his home, how he had developed video games before the Event. Like Isak, he had suddenly found himself in possession of an inexplicable ability: he could manipulate electronic devices using only his mind. All kinds of things, lights, telephones—

"What about a computer, do you have one of those?"

A slight pause. "Yes."

"You can use the Internet?"

Another pause. "Yes. But I don't."

"Why not?"

"I'm afraid," he spelled.

"Afraid of what?" May asked, though she felt that she already knew the answer.

"It'll be gone. It'll be blank. All of humanity's info lost."

"At least then we would know if we were back to square one," May sighed, walking over to the bookcase and running her fingers over the spines. Ed didn't answer.

"Do you have a TV?" Ed asked one day. He was on speakerphone, May and Isak sewing up holes in a set of jeans with dental floss. "May I?" A soft explosion of static zigzagged out of the TV set, so long silent in the corner of their living room. "Want to watch a movie?" Ed spelled, but May had already run to the cabinet where they kept all their DVDs. Isak was laughing softly.

"*I don't care, I'm still free,*" she sang, Isak joining in. "*You can't take the sky from me.*"

Despite the increased electrical presence in the house, transmitting scenes of spaceships and space cowboys swearing in Chinese, the level of buzzing in May's head didn't change. She could always tell when Ed was calling moments before the phone rang, as if she was watching him travel through the line toward them from a far-removed distance. Odd, she thought. Maybe the headaches weren't caused by electricity, but by something else.

Isak settled his arm around her as they took in the other voices and other faces, pictures that lessened some long unexpressed need that had slowly, slowly choked them. May looked up at Isak's face. It had been three days since his last skip forward. The swelling in his legs had decreased and his expression was less full of worry.

As the episode ended, Ed sent three pulses through the telephone.

"You were watching too?"

"Yes."

"We have the whole season. We've probably watched it... How many times would you say, Isak?"

"Three? Maybe once before we were married, too."

"Weird. I don't remember that."

Isak studied her hand, frowning slightly. "Your hands still aren't healed all the way over."

"No..."

"Hands?" Ed asked.

"When the stairs collapsed, the night everything disappeared, I hurt my hands trying to get Isak out of the mess. A lot of the boards had split, there were nails. Both his legs were chewed up pretty bad, I think one of them was fractured. He was unconscious. I had to lift a piece of railing off of him, not knowing if he was alive or dead. I didn't even really know what I was doing..." May upturned a palm on her lap, dim pink scars and a few fresh-looking cuts jumbled in her skin. "They're fine, though. Don't stop me from doing much."

"You haven't been bandaging them. They might get infected." Isak started ripping a strand of cloth off of his shirt.

"They will if I put that on it," she teased. "Don't worry." May suddenly felt incredibly sad. "Ed? Are you doing all right?"

"Yes."

"We should really try to figure out where you live, in case we ever want to visit."

Ed had developed a way of laughing in code: one long beep followed by two short ones. "HA ha ha," he said.

It was the last phone call they ever had.

Chapter Nine

Crack

Bone-sick weary, with split soles and worn-through faces, two walking ghosts collapsed next to a dilapidated shack, too many times fooled by hallucinations to believe it was there.

"Looks so real." Pinot's voice cracked and sputtered; they had been days without drink since happening on an abandoned truck with a half-empty six pack in the backseat, and those cans had drained fast. "Can we go in?" Pinot asked, crawling over to Miller and collapsing into his lap. "There will be something nice in the cupboards, I'm sure there will be something nice."

"This is all just a dream," he said, absently running his hand along her back. "It's always been a dream. Go if you want to. It's not real."

It was agony picking herself off his legs, crawling on her hands and knees toward the unhinged door. There were white lines and cracks in her arms, her flesh covered in calluses and flaking pieces of dead skin. It hurt to move. Pinot kept on, dragging her boots along the resilient ground in long scrapes, placing her palms flat, one in front of the other. Her dark eyes were huge in her wasted face; her throat was always in the process of trying to swallow so that her chin was constantly back against her neck. Her line of travel was mindless, the shack growing before her, the olive green walls graffitied over with pictures of brooding hipsters and magpies. The windows were boarded, the porch full of holes, with a wicker lounge chair crammed into the corner. A flash of an old lady seemed to sit in the chair, but when Pinot turned her full gaze onto it with a gasp, the vision was gone.

She placed a hand, shaking, onto the first wooden step, the natural rough-hewn grain embedding into her skin. The moment was somehow holy, and she remained there, with her eyes closed, communing with the long dead piece of tree that had been walked on day after day without ever really being noticed. The next step was acknowledged, her exhausted body groaning under the sustained altitude of her climb. The deck was made up of more substantial boards, though some had rotted through long ago and all of them had been bleached by the elements of an earlier world. Pinot pushed off the ground, placing her knees on the top step, proceeding upward. Once her hands and knees had met, she laid face down on the deck with her arms spread and her nose inhaling remnants of dust.

This is the most stable imaginary porch I've ever been on, she thought, before pressing forward. Her knees locked, she ached, she was moving not out of a measured, active decision, but some force of mind or will that kept telling her, "Go" — a mantra that she could bend to, and by obeying and repeating it in her mind could crawl one inch further and then another and then another—

She was brought up short by the bang of the door collapsing inward, shifted off balance by her added, though inconsequential, weight on the porch. A cloud of sawdust puffed up and settled gently into her hair as she crawled through the entrance.

Smooth and bare, the concrete floor was cool under her hands. Piles of sawdust were left around the room, stacks of lumber against the walls. A workshop bench with a rusted metal toolbox and empty coffee cups, stacks of unopened envelopes and a handsaw. An icon, depicting three figures seated in front of a gold background, hung on the back wall next to a closed closet door.

Pinot crawled toward it, her hands leaving streaks in the fine layer of sawdust. She reached up for its handle, pulling herself to her knees and unhooking the latch. Unsteady on her feet, she used the door to support herself as it swung outward. Inside the closet was a top shelf packed with drooling paint cans, a ball chain swinging from a cobwebbed light bulb, and from the clothes hangers—

"Hell, yes," Pinot whispered. Before her was by far the best part of the mirage so far. She grabbed a handful of the stuff and stumbled madly out of the shack, holding the strips of dried jerky up to Miller as if offering a sacrifice.

"Where did you get that?" he asked, gaping.

"It was a closet, not a cupboard," she allowed, throwing one into his lap. In a burst of energy, she ripped at a piece with her teeth, chewing with open lips.

Miller, too, fell to eating. Never had he seemed so wolfish in Pinot's eyes, as he tore into the dried-out meat. "Salty," he said, picking a bite out of his teeth. "Is there anything else in there?"

"You won't believe it." Pinot shook her head, pulling him up. "It's stocked, like a bomb shelter or something."

"What else is there?" Miller asked, his mouth hanging open.

"Beer, jerky, crackers, soup..."

They staggered up the steps, hurrying onto their plot of plenty, barely registering their cracked feet oozing in their boots. Miller went to his knees in the doorway of the closet, swinging his pack onto the floor next to him. "Settle in," he directed. "We'll be staying for a while."

Pinot jumped onto the workbench and kicked the toolbox onto the floor for joy.

—— «()» ——

When their stake ran out, Miller wanted to leave immediately.

"Gotta keep one step ahead of them," he mumbled, packing up two bottles of beer, a package of dried raisins, and the rest of the jerky. Stepping over the drained cans and the smashed beer bottles, Pinot followed him out of the shack, hesitating on the last stair.

"Hey Miller, do we have to? I kinda like this place. Nobody's bothered us, we still have some food left. Or, once we find another haul, bring it back here, hey? What d'you think?"

Miller kept walking.

Chapter Ten

Break

"A zombie apocalypse, that would've been interesting." Isak chewed through a piece of beef jerky, unearthed from some forgotten corner of the pantry. "We would've had to find a way to get all our supplies upstairs; they wouldn't be able to make it up to us there."

"The worst part would be having to listen to them moaning all day, and running into things, and not being able to do anything."

"We'd read Shakespeare aloud just to catch a break."

"Would they hang around or leave?"

"There has to be some way to get them out."

"They only want one thing. Would they be content with anything else?"

"I wonder if their obsession with brains has a metaphorical basis?"

"Maybe a mass cultural fear?"

"There are no zombies of any kind left in the world these days."

"How do you know? Maybe when we're asleep tonight, they'll crawl in through the kitchen window—"

"—and the monsters under the bed will chew through the rug and make terrible belching noises."

"Now you're just being ridiculous," May said in a voice she meant to sound injured but turned into laughter.

"It's almost worse this way," Isak stated, rubbing his leg thoughtfully. "Nothing to fight against. The environment's benign, we only know of one other person who may not even be alive—"

"He'll call again," May said with conviction.

"I pray for that every day. But the fact is, May, we're already going crazy here and—"

"What do you mean?"

"It's just been us for so long, in one small place. Sometimes I feel like if I don't get up and go somewhere—"

"Where, Isak? Where should we go? Even if we could find Ed, it wouldn't last long. Your legs..."

"They're strong enough. And I can always skip ahead if—"

"No landmarks," May continued. "We don't even know if the magnetic poles are in the same place. Everything's changed. Except this." She indicated the confines of the room, sweeping her arms. "And this." She gripped his arm as she kissed him.

"We can't stay here." Isak shook out his legs and stood slowly. "What'll we do when we run out, when the pantry's empty? Noah had years to stock up, and a family to share it with. What's the point of going on, May, if we don't affect anything? We need to find somewhere else to make our existence matter."

"I would rather die here." May stared into the Impressionistic painting. "Do you think the world committed suicide?" she asked, turning back toward Isak with a catch in her voice. "Do you think it had enough abuse and took its own life rather than go on being mistreated? I'm sorry, that was a stupid—"

"The world can't make a choice like that. God is the sustainer of life, all life."

May shook the rest of her apology out of her hands. "Did he give the go ahead then?"

"He said he wouldn't, a long time ago."

"But here we are, Isak."

"Yes."

May sank onto the coffee table, leaning her back against the wall and looking sideways out the window. It seemed to her that the glass was vibrating with the force of invisible sound, the energy of disembodied voices. "I can't go out there anymore. It's too loud." May stopped herself from going on, but Isak seemed not to have heard her. She had been asking questions for so long, trying to keep him in the moment, keep his mind off of the future, where any number of possibilities could draw him forward and leave her behind, that she had neglected her own answers. Were they the same as Isak's? May approached the world tentatively, while Isak considered it in poetic tones with bursts of melancholy passion. His heart, so inclined to optimism and compassion, was dampened by the cloud of vapors that could descend in the midst of his most earnest joys. Would her approach bring her to the same conclusions as Isak's wilder plunge into the universe? She wondered what Ed thought of all this, the Event, the land, his solitary existence. At least she had Isak; at least they had water, somewhere to live. Why did Isak want to leave all of it behind? Didn't he realize that they would never make it?

They had a truck, a '92 Ford that had horrible gas mileage and not enough cab space. If they tried to take that out and a tire burst or the battery died, they'd be dead in the water. But even if they could make it to Ed, would he be able to run the combustion engine and get them all back home, restocked, and with more hope? What if they made it, and found his body curled in a rotten fetal position next to an empty bag of potato chips? They could bury him. May would bring a paint stick to mark his grave.

"Don't think like that," she whispered to herself, but again Isak was deaf to her. He was considering something of his own, his brow contracted, his arms crossed over his chest. He was tied up in a motley brown housecoat, his bandaged legs sticking out from the hem like two kite spindles. He was right, they were getting stronger, finally. Was it normal for injuries to take so long to heal? She rubbed her hands, one over the other, snags of flesh catching on her wedding ring. Tea. Some tea would be nice right now. She left the living room, softly, placing one foot down in a steady decline starting from her heel to her toe, followed by the second. Isak stirred himself, looking at her from over the back of the couch.

"Where are you going?" he asked.

"Heating some water."

"Do you have to? It's hot enough in here already."

May bristled. "I was going to make some for you. Don't you know tea cools you down? They used to drink it in the desert..." An image of a man with a long beard squatting in front of a canvas tent in the Sahara, one hand on his white turban, the other emerging from a bundle of robes to pick up a small clay cup of tea. She shook it from her mind, her lips hot and parched. "I'm going outside anyway." She stormed into the kitchen, Isak wordless behind her. *Probably rubbing his chin*, she thought in disdain. The tier of drawers rattled as she pulled open the cupboard and retrieved the solar oven she had made out of aluminum foil and an umbrella. Since the rain, the gray disc of sky had lightened, allowing more diffused sunlight through to the earth. Instead of burning fuel, May could catch some of it and use it for heat. She sent the backdoor swinging, setting the concave device holding an aluminum dish full of water on an old deck chair. It wouldn't boil, of course, just get hot enough to draw the weak tea out of the crisp, dried out filters.

The sound outside reminded her of Ed, the spark that would go off in her head when he called. The stifling air crackled and yawned in a disturbing way, but, angry now, May sent a wild "Oh!" into the emptiness. Her paint sticks stood like a far-off forest of dead trees.

Chapter Eleven

Theories

What Ed had found. He sat back from the series of articles he had cut out from the stacks of old newspapers in the back room, gripping his shrunken stomach. Could it really be what he thought it was?

We just keep messing it up, he thought, pulling the feature describing the planned space-repair operation that he had ripped out of a mid-March copy of the *Globe and Mail*. His first clue had been the bill brought up for consideration in a UN meeting. It had passed with the full support of China, Australia, Great Britain, Canada, and Russia, but the details of the proposed mandate were hazy. He picked up another article, this one describing how the United States, still considered a leader in space travel, was convinced to sign onto the deal, the Patch Project. Arms may have traded hands, another government promising to give up nuclear projects if the U.S. would agree to dedicate their research and operational resources to the Patch cause.

Those were amongst hundreds of reports that Ed had found, on global warming, the polar ice caps, changes in atmospheric pressure and components, the slowing down of the thermohaline cycle, increased instances of cancer in Australia. Considering all those concerns, which had been on the backs of major world powers for the past seven decades, Ed was able to piece together what the purpose of the Patch Project was.

"It's unbearable!" he shouted to the assembled characters in his mind, slapping a hand on the imaginary podium. "We produce greenhouse gases, accelerating the build-up of carbon dioxide, and so on, in the atmosphere. There is a significant break down in the make-up of the ozone layer. Australia's right under that hole. Governments propose an internationally funded and run operation to patch it up, nice and tight, so that we can all go on with our lives, eating chocolate and whatever we damn well feel like! But! Oh, then..."

Something had gone wrong. Something had fallen through. The assembly went up in a ship, they attacked the hole with chemicals, seeing what would stick and what wouldn't. And then...

"Everything was vaporized. Everything except this little patch here of mine, and one patch for May and Isak. And if we survived, then who's to say there aren't any other patches out there. Patch Project, ha."

Ed rounded the far end of the counter and walked out on it all, into the wasteland, sterile and chemically neutralized by humanity's well-intentioned blunder. There was nothing in the air except eerie clouds that held themselves aloof from the matters of the earth. They had never seemed so far away in Ed's eyes.

One perk of having the lonely roadside convenience store at his disposal was the stash of DVDs, mindless fiction, and cheap impulse items. Porn too, hidden under the counter. They had been his way out at the start, but he was bored of all of it. He wanted real stories, real life to make sense to him, stripped of fantasy and power structures. His writing had helped him. Quality time in his mind had helped him. Loss was something he now understood, as he never had, cushioned in a million-dollar life. Before the Event, his family had always been distant, his friends moved on to other things, and he just kept pushing himself and pushing himself, past it all. But living out of a highway gas station, how could he not be faced with the inevitable: he was entirely alone.

Except for May and Isak. But how could he tell them what he had discovered? It made him sick to think about. He had to process it all, think of the best way to tell them his theory.

Katherine, he thought suddenly. *Maybe she's still alive.* He wasn't sure if it even mattered to him anymore. It was all so distant, as if it had happened long ago in some unconquered and antiquated society. Future generations would discover artifacts, houses, skeletons, the very few tendrils of them clinging to the linoleum after the broom of time had swept up the rest.

Katherine had been an archeologist. She could put names to rocks on Pacific beaches, ramble on about the Aztecs or the Romans through a five-course dinner. Someone who had traveled to the outer reaches of the Andromeda Galaxy would make him feel the same way. Small. Ignorant. Self-inflated. Katherine collapsed him like a puzzle box just by raising her eyebrows.

Something else had driven him out of the familiar circle of the gas station. Katherine was dead. Karl, who had dislocated his collarbone and given him a concussion, was dead. And he had finally remembered why he was in the phone booth that night: he had pulled over, drunk, with a number written on his arm, to call a fourteen-year-old who was now also deceased. This should have filled him with horror, with sadness and loss, but he felt as if it was all over years ago and had actually happened to someone else. That he had lived alone his whole life, surrounded by junk food and locked-up packages of cigarettes, dreaming up stories and delusions of a past existence.

He thought about walking to the end of the sky to see if it was painted drywall and everything a set up. Were they using drugs on him, suppressing his natural emotions? No, he didn't need third-party scientists messing up his life: it was all him. He stopped, his hands clenched child-like in the pockets of his jacket, and mouthed his own name: Ed.

Chapter Twelve

Light to the West

Isak reclined on one elbow, studying the underside of the padded seat of the antique chair that sat next to the front door. The chair was for tying shoes on, for quick reposes and transitory stays. No one ever contemplated in the entryway chair or used it for fun. It was an eye piece mostly, with its curved and fancy-footed legs, white and gold painted wood framing the rich red, and ivory scrolls decorating the seat. Shifting his weight back toward his hips, Isak followed the delicate weave of a spider web around to the front of the chair. "He's a small guy. Can hardly make him out."

"Where?" May crouched down behind him, peering into the murky corner.

Isak traced a glint of spider web. "I wonder how long he's been at it."

"Industrious." May grinned, picking out the speck that floated from behind where the leg and seat joined.

"A big job for anyone," Isak agreed.

They watched the spider cross, seeming to float from one chair leg to the other, in mild admiration, its work so small and so important.

"I wonder if he'll catch anything," May said darkly, sitting back on her heels and thinking of the dead, empty space that surrounded them on all sides.

"At least he's trying," Isak said, reaching back for her hand without taking his glance from the web. "Look at how invested he is."

"He doesn't know what we do. He doesn't see the world the way we do. Maybe he wouldn't keep going if he did."

"Maybe if we saw the way he did, we would understand."

May raised the back of his hand to her lips. "What have we missed?" she asked.

Isak shrugged, and pushed himself to his feet. "I feel lazy watching him," he said. "How about a walk?"

"A walk?" May laughed. "We haven't been on a walk since..."

"Why not?"

May paused, wondering if now was the best time to tell him about the outdoor buzzing. "It's, well, I guess it would be good for your legs—"

"I'm tired of being bedridden! I could run a mile by now, I think." He winked at her.

"Put some pants on first," she said, tugging down the edge of his housecoat and patting his bare calf, the skin still pink, but almost whole.

It was like getting a three-year-old ready to go to the park. Isak hobbled excitedly around the living room, gathering socks, runners, a loose pair of brown dress pants. The shirt under his housecoat was crumpled with spots of tea down the front. His hair was on the long side, black and tangled. "Do you have everything?" May asked as he took her arm, grinning.

"We're just going for a walk," Isak said, as they pulled the door closed, tucking the house key in May's back pocket.

They turned left despite the fact there were no roads to follow. The rippled landscape, pockmarked by rain and dried crisp by the afternoon sun, passed under their feet and extended in front of them, a constant now, that left no sign of their passing. They made a wide circle, keeping their house always in the peripheral as Isak's breathing became harsher, his steps less confident. May tried to keep her expression cheerful, her voice bright, despite the static in her ears. "I've been meaning to say thank you," she told him. "You've stayed with me, even though you could have skipped all of this..."

"Yes. I could have. But life is life, May. How could I waste a second of it, when so many others didn't make it this far?"

"What do you think we should do with it? Life, I mean."

Isak stopped a moment, rubbing his eyes and straightening his back. "Create something."

May felt her stomach clench, a bad memory.

He looked into her eyes, the line of bronze in his seeming to almost glow in the weird outdoor light. "I mean, whatever we're supposed to make, whether that's art or history or even just thought itself."

"You're such a poet," May acknowledged, releasing her breath.

"You didn't used to think much of that."

She nodded, curling a piece of hair around her finger. "Seems ridiculous now." She pulled at the strand, the buzzing coming to a crescendo around her, in a deluge of half-voiced crying, like of a small child over the hum of electrical wires, and then—

"Get down!" she screamed, pulling Isak to the ground. An explosion of light bleached the landscape white, spraying past her closed eyelids as the torrent of unidirectional sound deafened her ears. The earth was sharp under her forearms, and she prayed that she hadn't done any more damage to Isak's legs by taking him down so violently.

Her second hearing, as she had taken to calling it, returned to its usual outdoor setting, a persistent jumble running through her temples. She realized now that the light itself wasn't anything to be afraid of. She lifted her face toward the far-off point where bright spurts were still escaping into the atmosphere. "Okay ... okay..." She sat up, waiting for Isak to recover himself. His arm was still over his eyes, small bits of dirt embedded into skin.

"What was that?" he gasped, remaining as if frozen.

"I don't know." May scanned the horizon, honing in on the slip of light before it was sucked back past her line of sight. "It hurt someone. I could hear her."

Isak lowered his arm. "You heard something?"

"Why didn't you skip ahead?" she asked, almost accusingly.

"I was caught in the moment," he said. "I was scared."

May stood up, trying to detangle the buzzing. "I thought you could hear it too. After the Event, it was constant, it was everywhere. Louder outside. I thought you could hear it too."

"I couldn't."

"Do you think it's because of what happened... Your time traveling? Maybe I picked up something too. I just don't know what it means."

Her sight was blurred around the edges, from light shock. Isak was blinking rapidly, trying to clear his vision. May helped him to his feet, absently brushing dirt from her charcoal blouse and his torn t-shirt. If she listened more attentively, perhaps she could make out where it was coming from.

"May?" Isak looked apologetic.

"Go ahead." She nodded, noticing the darkening red spots soaking through his knees. She blinked and he was gone. Before returning home, May tried to find the voice that had cried out before the onslaught of light, but it too had disappeared out of time.

Chapter Thirteen

Power

Pinot and Miller circled the structure, a jumble of black iron and twisted steel cables. Encased in a chain-link cage, the wires at acute angles to the concrete pad grounding it, the power station seemed like some kind of ancient captured monster, trapped for weary centuries, with ten-towered horns and thousands of securing bolts for unblinking eyes.

"O, great and powerful, how you have fallen." Miller threw a rusted piece of pipe metal into the compound. They both heard it clatter to rest in the unseen belly of the dead electric god.

"Are you named?" Pinot continued, rattling the fence, her dark, cracked nails grasping the metal wires. "Zeus? Chaos? Moloch?"

"Or are you the spirit of your founder, Tesla, locked in machinery?"

"Either way, you are dead! No more all-seeing overlord traveling on waves through the air! No more power behind security cameras and Big Brother screens! No more garish light to expose our deeds!"

Miller leaped, wedging his boots and hands through the empty diamonds in the fence, ascending.

"Where are you going, Miller?" Pinot left the iron bar she was trying to free from the ground, following behind him.

"There might be others," he said, landing heavily on the other side. "They'll want to use this place like they did before. Resurrect the thing."

"The shell must be destroyed," Pinot apprehended. "And the ghost inside it."

This is what they had dreamed of: complete destruction beyond vandalism or public mischief. Something really moving. *We're moving mountains*, Pinot thought. O victorious thought, thought full of disdain for the weak who clung to the safety of order. "You people who are afraid of everything, who deny yourselves!" she shouted as she landed next to Miller. "You pursuers of wealth! You cacti of salted deserts, hoarding water and just surviving. You would take my freedom and spit in my face. We will crumple you forever—"

Her cheek, the right one, turned hot, her body contorting from force of impact. She tasted blood in her mouth, her eyes burst with blindness. She recovered herself, back against the fence, Miller shaking the fist from his hand.

"You talk too much."

Pinot gasped and tasted rust in the air. She could feel the puffiness in her cheek where Miller had struck her. For the first time in her life, she wished she were dead.

"Fucker! Who said you could do that?" she yelled to his back.

"Nobody. Nobody told me anything." Miller bent down and slowly rose with a conglomerated chunk of concrete in his hand. "And if they did," he said, turning toward Pinot, "I wouldn't listen." He slammed the piece with a crash into a secured panel, crumpling the lock. A column of switches and a copper plate which Miller soon pried free; he twisted wires apart, crossed them, flipped one by one the thick plastic toggles. "Come on, Pinot. Flip a fucking switch."

There was one, at the bottom, still pointing left. Pushed over, it would look just like the others. It would be uniform. The same. She watched her hand, the iron rose gleaming on the third finger, as it reached for the warm plastic toggle.

"Do it." Miller was leaning behind her, the weight of his body against her back.

From somewhere deep in the reaches of her inner world, Pinot saw a gleam in the deep, some silver in the tar sands. And reaching down toward it, with Miller's breath on her neck, she found a hook. A left hook.

It took him square in the ear, evoking a cry of rage as one of his dreads soaked up the brown-red spray of blood. His fingers explored the membrane and came away wet. His face spoke death as he licked each digit clean. "Come here."

Pinot crumpled in against the switchboard, her dry mouth tingling with fear. "That man," she rasped. "That man said…"

"Shut up!"

"…you have another name… He said your name is Cauldor."

"I'm going to fucking kill you!" Miller screamed, propelling himself toward her, his hand reaching for her throat. Pinot ducked, smelling burned flesh as Miller became the grounding wire for the open panel of cables he had activated. She crawled along the unfriendly concrete, trying to escape the crackling behind her, the unearthly buzz that wowed in and out, louder and louder, the havoc culminating in a whine that turned into white fire as the structure melted into itself. Pinot, her palms and soles tingling, her mouth dripping blood, a forgotten bruise on her neck shining purple and blue, discovered in that moment that she very, very much wanted to live.

Chapter Fourteen

Desert

The first time Ed ran away from home, he was nine. Looking for Dad because Mom had kicked the bastard out for good this time, the wandering drunk with a briefcase hastily packed full of sketchbooks and spare socks. Ed found out later that his dad had taken a bus to Kitchener, where his aunt lived.

When he was fourteen, meeting his dad at a hotel downtown, Ed watched as the stranger across from him downed glass after glass of Rickard's Red.

"How can you do that to yourself?" Ed needled, scooping a mouthful of soggy green peas. He frowned at the waitress who had just set down another half-sleeve.

"That's what you think?" his dad chortled thickly. "You're a kid. You don't know what it's like to have the weight of the world on your shoulders, with everyone wanting something out of you, when you got nothing to give. Hey, Eddie." His dad gripped him by the arm. "Don't turn out like those punks your age, smoking whatever shit they smoke, and dropping out of school. You need an education. That's something I never had, and now look at me. Living on scraps and slouching along, too tired to get out of bed most days. I'm tired. I've been sucked dry by life, Eddie. I gotta quench that desert somehow."

For years, Ed was angry. He stopped answering phone calls, regardless of whose name appeared on the call display. Once he graduated high school, he grabbed his pack and was out in the world, hitchhiking across Europe and trying to find a way out. He found Maggie. They had a good run. She set him up at an animation studio, in-betweening at first. But he was determined, worked his way up. They paid him good money and he got to do what he loved most: tell stories, stories he had never been able to tell anyone before, about mysterious wanderers with socks in battered leather briefcases and lonely women standing at kitchen sinks that their tears filled to the brim.

Suddenly, Ed was brought back into the present moment, spinning a slow 360, taking in the panorama of wasteland. He listened again. Voices? Out here? Where were they coming from? Ed turned toward the sound and made out the shape of some kind of building or structure, rearing out of the earth. He began to run toward it, identifying it as a power station, all the latticed towers and playground feel of space and metal under hands. Before he reached it, a flare of white light filled the sky, nearly blinding him (*Great*, he thought, *blind and mute now*), the metal melting down, a chaotic watercolor with heat and crackling noise, like someone rubbing a sheet of wax paper against itself. Screaming? Where was it coming from?

Instead of hitting the ground, which may have been the smarter thing to do, Ed pressed on, shading his eyes with his hand, though the dazzling light had been sucked away, leaving the faint gray daylight. He blinked rapidly as he approached the compound, trying to clear his vision. The chain-link was ruptured from the meltdown; he slipped underneath a piece rolled back on itself, and recoiled. The black husk of what once had been a person slumped against a jagged post. Had that been the voice? But there it was again, this time quieter, a forlorn whimper silent enough to be air.

Hello? he mouthed, following the sound. He walked along the fence line, the hair-raising smell of charged air getting into his head, telling him to run. Instead, Ed leaned down over the scorched body of a young woman, picked her up, and made his way slowly out of the compound.

Chapter Fifteen

Dreams

Upstairs, the blinds were all closed. May turned slowly, glancing past the door frames into dark rooms, the walls blank. Her painting at the top of the stairs was missing. She started to back down from the doors crowding inward, but her foot hit air and she felt a sickening falling feeling in her stomach. Right. The stairs had collapsed. She grasped the walls on either side of her, keeping herself from falling as Isak had, onto the jagged floorboards sticking up from below. How had she gotten here? It felt like the middle of the night, with the dim shapes and the distorted perspective. Sometimes at night, she had looked to the window, watching the window frame bend and expand, but somehow never break, car headlights gleaming across the ceiling.

"There are no more cars," she told herself, turning down the hall and entering what used to be their bedroom. It was above the living room, their queen-sized bed situated in the center, surrounded by bookcases, an easy chair, a scattering of open books, and an overturned basket of laundry. She drew close to the bed, a crawling sensation starting at the base of her neck and running up into her hairline. Suddenly, she didn't want to see what was lying there, in a twisted, shadowy, and human-looking pile. Her hands reached out on their own, pulling back strips of rags and old clothes, until before her was a tiny face mounted on a tiny body. It opened its eyes and whispered something, but she didn't hear it, she was screaming and covering her ears and throwing the clothes back over top of it. "You're dead!" she told it, shaking her head and trying to run. Her legs were gone. She was lying on top of a mound with a paint stick through her heart, watching a wave slam their house into kindling sticks. Isak wavered in and out of her vision. "I have to go," was all he said, pulling tenderly at her hair. She caught a scent of something: soap, and cherry blossoms. She opened her eyes again and found herself in front of a monumental coil with electrical wires flinging out of it in all directions, poled power lines that led off along the barren landscape, some double-u-ing off into space. The *buzz-crackle-hum* of the generator was close to deafening. She ran all along the chain-link fence built around it thinking, *How do I turn it off, how do I turn it off?*

She sensed someone running after her. "Ed?" she stopped, turning around. A man dressed in a navy pinstripe suit stood behind her, his face a dialing pad. "Dali?" HA ha ha! he beeped. He was spelling something to her, but it was too fast. "Slow down," she begged. "I don't understand! We have to find Isak," she told the telephone man. "He's looking for the books he lost." It all made sense to her now. They would go to the library, he would be there, in his fraying tweed coat that was too old for him. They walked for hours before May remembered that the library and everything else was gone.

"Who are all those people?" she asked; the Dalian pointed toward them as if to say, "Keep looking." They were monstrous, in size, proportion; they carried in their hands fire and cans of paint, looking for holes in the sky that sucked up the dry ground and splintered light into pixels. They reached up to fit the holes back together and weld them shut, sealing them with a white layer from their brushes and rollers. But then they began arguing, yelling in every language, loudly, louder! One hit another. They forgot their cans and handfuls of fire, dropping them. The cans and fire fell, all catching alight before hitting the ground in a catastrophic crash that bleached everything white: the sky, the giants who had frozen as statues, everything except May and the Dalian who stood alone on the top of a hill, surrounded by bones that had been bleached by a thousand years.

———— ⟨⟩ ————

May sat up. Isak lay on her right, face turned toward her, his thin shoulders sticking up at odd angles. Her senses were strangely acute, her pulse rapid, she could feel it pounding in her ears. What kind of nightmare was that? She didn't want to delve into symbols, not now when horror pumped vinegar through her insides. Isak might find it interesting, in the morning.

She lay back, adjusting her head to rest more comfortably on the flattened pillow. Sleep did not return. Images of the undead child and the generator leaped up to her mind; she shook her head, telling herself it was only a dream. They weren't eating enough, that was the reason, her brain was starting to short circuit. That in itself was frightening. She half-wished everything was over so she didn't have to feel so sad. She turned onto her stomach, wrapping her arms around herself, closing her eyes. The wave hit the house again and again and again, as she forced herself into sleep.

"Isak," she said the next morning as she poured the last of the tea into a tiny clay mug. "You're right. It's time to leave."

Chapter Sixteen

Full Circle

Her palms were blasted through, the soles of her feet raw. A stray current had used her body like a switch, closing the circuit between sky and earth. Her hair was half burned off, her eyelids were swollen and red. Two pale pink lines of new skin streaked down from them like pathways. Spots of the same color were on her arms.

Ed didn't know much about medicine, but he had studied survival skills once to help with a futuristic war game he was developing. He ripped off what clothing hadn't been seared to her body. He removed her runners. Her black jacket was completely fused along her shoulders, the collar cradling her bruised neck. It wasn't long before he realized that this woman should be dead.

The walk back to the convenience store was agonizing, the woman starting sometimes, or mumbling, or screaming without opening her eyes. Ed was out of shape from staying so close to the gas station. Short of breath, he stopped a couple times, sinking to the ground with the body still in his arms. The eventual sight of the ugly siding and the grungy silhouettes of the gas pumps in the fading evening light was enough to bring a sense of homecoming and resolution back into his stride. He turned on the red neon "SUPINA MERCANTILE" sign along the roof of the building with his mind.

Almost there now, sweetheart, he thought to the woman, blowing a cool stream of air onto her forehead. *Why'd I do that?* he thought, suddenly ashamed. *She's not a kid. She's dying.*

Inside, Ed thought the lights on. He thought the ice machine to its highest setting. He swept the articles and papers he had found off the front counter; they fluttered, confused, to the floor in a flat jumble, some slouched against the side of the sliding glass door of the refrigerator. He placed the woman on the glass countertop, pulling off his canvas jacket and bundling it under her head.

Anti-bacterial wipes were his first thought, followed by hundred milliliter packages of burn cream and rolls of gauze off of the back rack. He filled a large plastic bin with ice and lowered the woman into it.

She's going to die... She's going to die...

A vision of little Hannah in her Christmas dress danced in front of his eyes.

He sanitized his hands, slapping the excess onto his face as he leaned down with his ear suspended over the burned woman's mouth, counting the space between breaths. He felt a strange compulsion to open one of her eyes. Gently, he pushed her swollen eyelid back. The iris was dark and rich, so deep brown it was almost black, skipping up, down, side to side in erratic REM jerks. He hid it from sight, frightened almost that she was in the middle of a revelation. He had written a character like that once, an Elven battle princess who would fall into trances and reveal to men the secrets of their hearts. If she was anything like that child of his mind, she would not take kindly to having her eye pried open.

A stutter ran through her body and a deluge of blood and mucus burst out of her nose. *Damn,* he thought, tearing the solid plastic cover off a roll of gauze.

Like most people he had known, Ed conceived of God as a universal principle that existed but was too mysterious, not even a being, a He or She or What, but an energy that couldn't be appealed to or offended because it was without identity. But at this moment, the idea of God suddenly became painfully personal. *Don't let this happen,* he thought, fitting two cloth pieces into her nostrils. He used a microfiber dishcloth to gently rub some of the blood from her face and the collar lying flat next to her ear. The ragged jacket flared black between her and the ice like the promise of death.

He searched around for something else he could use. Q-tips, mousetraps, sewing kits (his stomach flipped at the thought of stitches in flesh), lady pads, shampoos, green gallons of aloe vera gel. He pulled two bottles off the shelf, one in each hand, running back to the woman. He unscrewed the white ridged cap and pried off the white sealing circle, oozing some of the stuff onto his fingers. It smelled exotically medicinal.

He traced the pink lines down her face, spreading the gel over her cheeks, down to the repulsive flakes on her neck. His mother had done the same to him once, after he had swum an hour in a friend's outdoor pool, diving underwater whenever she appeared at the side, a thick blue bottle of sunscreen in her hand.

The woman's lips were bruised but not black; they could even be considered normal, untouched by the force which had vanquished most of her body. The pink streaks, and the pink lips, they were almost new looking...

——— «» ———

A dim sense of sound from somewhere far away heightened into the grumbling hum of a truck engine. Ed's eyes blinked open. His first impulse was to check on the woman. The roar of the approaching vehicle grew louder as he kneeled beside her. No change. Her breathing had steadied over the past three days, but she was still unconscious. The engine slowed and idled. Still next to her, he thought on the screen behind the counter that tellers had once used to monitor gas pumps. There was a truck all right, pulled into lane two, with two shady figures in the cab and a sheet bungee-corded over a full load of cargo, a stainless steel ladder hanging conspicuously out the tail end. Ed felt an urge to reach for a shotgun that wasn't there.

The driver jumped out and hurried to the passenger door. She was a fine boned, black-haired, emaciated woman. Caucasian, wearing a long jean jacket over a mauve and white knee length dress. Ed ran to the door, the bells overhead clanging wildly as he exited onto the step. *I'll be right back,* he thought. *I'll be right there.*

"I'll be right back," the driver was saying to the man in the passenger seat. "If it's not him, I'll—"

"Shh!" The man motioned to her. "I think I heard something."

They didn't move. They were listening. And then it came again. The sound of tapping. Five. And then Four. Their eyes flew toward the sound, the woman grasping the man's arm, a short laugh escaping from them both.

Ed was leaning against the gas pump, a hand raised and a shy smile on his exhausted face.

BOOK TWO

Chapter One

New Arrangements

Every morning, Isak and Pinot raced around the convenience store. Pinot often took the lead despite her scarred feet and the red skin on her hands, wrapped determinedly around the handles of Isak's old crutches. In May's opinion, the daily loop wasn't just exercise; it gave them some of the old joy of movement for movement's sake, that hint of self-sufficiency in being able to propel themselves forward through space. She told herself it was good, but she couldn't help feeling wary. Isak's leg was still stiff. May had made another ritual of rubbing down his calf every evening before everyone scattered for bed. They were set up in the storage room and slept on quilts Isak's grandmother had given them for their wedding, spread over a stack of flattened cardboard boxes. Ed slept on the doorstep or in the flatbed of the truck.

"I'd sleep there!" Pinot grimaced. She hated to be shown up by Ed, but with her skin still tender from the electric burns, the best place for her was indoors. She was restricted to a bench, pulled in from in front of the store, where old men had smoked and teenagers had consumed slurpees in the hot October dusk. "It smells like shit," she complained. Midnight would find her with a ragged piece of black cloth bunched under her head, refusing coverings of any kind. "They scratch me," she said.

Pinot stayed aloof, quiet at their sparse meals of chips, Gatorade, and the occasional piece of chocolate from the stash in the back. They had put most of the food away; out of sight, out of mind, behind the counter, in boxes stacked in the storage room. Isak, who had an injury to sympathize with, managed to draw Pinot into a game of chess once in a while. May, who had tended to Isak's leg and her own scars for long enough, considered Pinot's itchy skin with a doctoring eye and reminded her constantly not to scratch. Once May even tried to get her to wear cloth gloves; of course, Pinot only cut off all the fingers.

Pinot didn't talk to Ed at all.

— «» —

One afternoon was the same as another. The same untouched weather, the same dim shadows gathered around the gas pumps, the same depleted shelves looming like bare trees in wintertime. The same tiles, the same windows, the same looking for something, and the same exhausted hunger. Ed was starting to hate it. He sat on the counter, thinking up a scenario where an unarmed man was faced with an entire legion of Orcs. He worked through possibilities involving special powers, calling for backup, an unexpected act of mercy that undoes evil. But thinking realistically, the unnamed man would have to die.

He flipped switches on and off, explored some more dead-end telephone lines. He had run out of electronics. He was bored with the laptop and most of the fridges were empty.

With a sick jolt, he realized there was something else in the room that ran off electrical impulses. *No, he thought, that's not allowed*. The more the idea ran through his mind, however, the more he thought, what harm could it do, really? It's not like he'd be breaking anything.

Pinot was sitting on her bench with her legs stretched out, using a broken pencil to sketch out a figure on Isak's copy of *Catcher in the Rye*, May's art college sweater bunched over her stomach, her washed out jeans ripped open at the knees. Pinot winced as the raw skin on her forehead tried to furrow under the force of her concentration.

Ed didn't know much about biology. Something about synapses and gray matter, dendrites. He wondered how to begin and on his first tentative venture into her mind, inadvertently caused her left foot to twitch. Exhilarated, he shut his eyes, traveling the impossible network of her brain. He could create temporary bridges over the gaps, spin his mind through her skin. Did she even notice? After all, he was just looking. He explored the dizzying circuitry running through her body, fleeing the deadened nerve endings and their accompanying flashes of scent, like matches being struck. He avoided those reminders, chasing down his craving.

Pinot, swinging her legs down off the bench, the rips in the thighs of her jeans tightening over pink skin, swaying toward him, her head tilted coyly and her lips slightly parted. When Ed opened his eyes, she was right in front of him, posing just as he had fantasized, her hand reaching toward him. Wait. Not reaching—

"Whatever the hell you're doing you better stop, or I'll cut a smile into your throat!"

Ed groaned inaudibly, looking up through his newly blackened eye. Pinot was glaring down at him from over the counter, a knife in her hand. When he inhaled, he smelled sewage wafting up from the corner drain.

The bells over the door clamored, a set of hands pulled Pinot back out of his view, her cries of outrage slowing into a low rumble of words. Ed grabbed the edge of the counter and pulled himself up to standing. May was sitting next to Pinot on the bench, a hand on her shoulder, nodding as Pinot mumbled and stared at the empty hand in her lap. Ed had difficulty recognizing Isak, whose face was uncustomarily grim.

"What happened?"

It's not what you think, Ed replied with his hands, waving them over each other and shaking his head.

"Write it down."

Ed brushed him off with a voiceless laugh, air escaping through the side of his mouth in disdain. He made a show of pulling a roll of paper and pencil from the top drawer, beginning his epistle with a flourish. He wrote, scratched out, wrote more, sweat beginning to bead on his upper lip.

There. He presented the paper, throwing down the golf pencil. Isak picked it up and read over the paragraph without expression. Pinot, a seething shadow, appeared from behind Isak, grabbed the paper and scanned it with her teeth clenched.

"Ed," May said from a distance. "We're grateful that you're sharing your home with us. That's not in doubt. But — whatever you did to Pinot, it must never happen again. I understand, your ability is still strange and accidents happen, but unless you figure out how to control yourself— What I'm trying to say is that we can't stay with someone who— We have enough to deal with as it is. And Pinot, she's just a kid, Ed. Do you see what I'm trying to say?"

Ed nodded once, trying to catch Pinot's eye. *I want to say sorry, so that she'll hear me.* But, of course, he couldn't.

After that, Ed started going on long walks in the afternoons, and didn't eat much. One day, he didn't come back.

Chapter Two

Wilderness

In walking, he hoped to find some kind of revelation. Some path of deep thought that would change him enough to deserve their trust again. Across the rippled plain of zombie paradise, Ed wandered, feeling the tepid earth under his feet and the frayed edges of his sleeves. Nothing came except trivial inventories and snapshots of Katherine. And thirst. Sometimes he didn't think at all, getting lost in the gnawing inside him, his eyes memorizing the flat horizon and putty-colored earth.

When Ed had set out that morning, he hadn't intended to go very far. He never went far, always keeping the store in sight, wondering how the others were spending their time, time free from his presence. Ever since he had entered Pinot's circuitry, he had sensed a wariness toward him. Glances behind his back, eyes adverted, strained conversation. Pinot hid in May and Isak's room, reading. That was enough to drive him further, out to the east, feeling the distant sun pushing on his back. There was nowhere to go, nothing to see, nothing to hope for. Take nature out of the picture and humans have only themselves to strive against. The environment of society, taxes, rent, car payments, credit card bills, groceries, dates, tabs — with that gone, what was there to complete or master? Where could he go to escape himself?

Reaching a Lilliputian city of rocks, Ed sat on a flat piece of slate. He studied the ground between his feet, rubbing his hands through his hair, trying to loosen the thoughts, flinging them out into the desert. What was his problem? He had made a mistake, okay, he could accept that. Why did he keep kicking himself out of the house? May and Isak and Pinot, they were fine, they were over it, he saw that now. He'd just projected his own feelings onto them.

But then an image of May, looking at him, a protective arm around Pinot's shoulders, rose up in his mind. *No*, he sighed, *they don't trust me anymore. They think I'm a pervert. A selfish fuck who doesn't really care about anybody. A user.*

Maybe they're right, came to him. *I'm an utter piece of shit.*

That's it, he thought. *That's it. And I knew it all the time, I just didn't want to say it out loud.*

He wiped his dry lips with the sleeve of his canvas jacket. The cuffs of his gray jeans were frayed into strips and the soles of his leather shoes were starting to peel. Everything was going to pieces.

Maybe I should start heading back, he thought, but didn't move.

Light began to wash out, the setting sun pulling it away through the thick clouds like a tide. Vague shadows pulled out from the pebbles and from the bases of boulders, from Ed's curved figure, sitting motionless on the rock. Dim coolness, familiar to him because of his nights spent under the unbroken sky, settled in around him, but still he didn't move.

I can't go back, he thought. *How could I have thought that I could?*

Honestly, he asked himself, *you didn't realize what kind of person you were before? Think about it. That chain of one-night girls, drinking, sleazy lines, hack art, come on!*

But it's still my life. It's no worse than what everybody does — you think I can accept that all of it was a waste?

I can't go back.

A steady tapping, increasing in volume, woke Ed out of his thoughts. Footsteps were approaching him in the dark, but still he couldn't move. *Whatever it is, I don't care.*

A flare of light startled him, but he saw it was only a match. Someone was lighting a candle. It was in a lantern, one carved out of wood with panes of glass set into the sides.

"Don't be afraid," came a voice. There was enough light for Ed to make out a stocky figure with shoulder-length dark hair and a face expressing peace and goodwill. The man set the lantern on the ground between them. "Where are you going?" he asked, settling on a rounded boulder across from Ed.

Ed shrugged, then pointed to his throat, shaking his head.

"I see. I am afraid it has been difficult for you, hasn't it?"

It may have been that he hadn't eaten for days, but Ed started tearing up. *You have no idea.*

"It's all right. There's nothing wrong with tears." The man's brow was contracted with compassion. Ed thought he had never seen anyone look at him so sincerely before. That thought was just enough to push tears out of his eyes. They trailed down over his cheekbones, which only reminded him of Pinot. Everything in his heart was leading to something else until Ed was sobbing soundlessly into his hands.

"Why don't you go home?" he heard the old man say. "They're worried about you, I bet."

Ed took gulps of air, trying to steady his breath, wiping his eyes on the heels of his hands. After a couple minutes, once the river had run itself out and Ed found himself strangely refreshed, he raised his eyes on a vacant boulder and a landscape empty of life. The lantern glowed at his feet, but the kind old man was gone.

Chapter Three

Saint

Rain came, this time in a mist, a thickening of air that left drops on the windows. May was sitting cross-legged on the counter, eyes out of focus. Vagabond on the edge of her consciousness, she crawled through hazy memories and out-of-place ideals that glowed and split into atoms, like a drop of ink in a beaker of boiling water. The jarring sound of someone entering filled her mind and rang empty as the bells settled into silence. Ed was standing in the doorway, wiping droplets off his face with his sleeve.

"It's your fault," May whispered. "Isak's gone, and it's your fault."

Ed slouched against the glass wall, framed by the empty landscape dyed gray with moisture.

"After you left, Pinot ran off, and the stress was too much for him."

A few moments passed before Ed walked over to the counter and lifted a piece of receipt paper out of the drawer. *What are you talking about?* he wrote, placing his question in her upturned hand. May didn't move. Across from her was a Coca-Cola fridge with decals of pop prices glued to the glass door. One of them had been set slightly crooked: a $1.89 sticker for Mountain Dew. A faint shadow of Ed and May reflected back to them.

"Do I need to spell it out for you?" her voice demanded, low and dangerous and hurt. "Isak's gone." A sudden increase of rain pounding the roof startled them out of tension for a moment, May's breathing sounding in steady, measured beats. She sighed and turned her eyes to the tiled ceiling. "Maybe we should have told you, when he was still here. Even now I'm forgetting" — she smiled in a weak, apologetic way— "that not everyone knows what Isak can do."

Ed nodded, encouraging her to go on.

"We won't catch up to him for a while this time. I know him. He'd want to see both of you safely back here. Where did Pinot go, Ed?" she asked, breaking out of her grief enough to look at him.

He took her hand and raised the paper up to her eyes.

"Isak has an ability, like you, but different. His gift lets him skip forward in time. It's dependent on his desires. If he yearns for something enough, that yearning pulls him to that time in the future when it will be fulfilled. It's been ... very difficult for him to control. He has to fully live in the present, otherwise ... even when he gets tired enough, he'll blink and find himself in bed that evening. It's been better since we've been here, there're more things for him to focus on. I'm sorry, Ed. I know it's not because of you, this time. And I've had my share of guilt."

Ed scrawled another line, placed it in May's hand, then turned and walked out the door.

"Ed! Where are you..." May read the paper.

I know where she went.

———— ‹›› ————

At the electrical power center of what used to be a city, people used to say they could hear the voice of a child who died there while retrieving a Frisbee. There had been a huge uproar after the child's death. People had wanted the station closed, since it posed such a danger to the community. Petitions and posters had flooded the city; in the end, city council overturned a thousand signatures, promising better warning signs and Electrical Safety Education. The station had been allowed to continue functioning and, eventually, the story of the child who had died became a ghost tale. So it was that the same power station was thirty years old and twice a murderer the day it expired in a hell of melting aluminum.

Pinot stood in the middle of it, seeing and feeling and remembering the blast of heat and crawling electrical buzzing swarming around her. Sensations flowed, her face empty and lost. She had all that was left of Miller's black jacket wrapped around her neck like a scarf. Everything came in bursts. She wiped her lips; they were cracked and dry. *Would I kill for a bottle now?* she thought.

She remembered the shack where they had found a stockpile of food and beer, and the faces of the three figures in the icon by the door. It was so far away to her, four solid walls that someone had once used as a workshop. She lowered herself onto the ground and hugged her knees.

"Right here," she said, passing a hand over the wispy white hair that had started to come in where the rest had burned off. "What good is it trying to go on anyway?" She thought about Ed, wandering in the bleak outside, looking for his death too, maybe. She spun the rose ring around and around, flicking it faster and faster around her bony finger. She thought about the strange man she and Miller had met and why she had so wanted to kill him. Where was he now?

The death-scape dimmed. Another face came into focus in front of her, this one even more foreboding than her nightmares of Goldi-dreads and his cruel iron hands. It was a middle-aged man, with startlingly white teeth and a buzz cut. Pinot began to cry.

"Say, Pinot," said the talking head. "I've got something I think you're going to like."

"Fuck off," Pinot whispered between breaths. She buried her face deeper into her knees, but the head kept talking.

"You're a pretty young lady, aren't you, Pinot? I can make you feel like you are."

Something new was happening in Pinot's stomach. Instead of the chaotic pangs of fear or the boiling bile of hatred, she felt herself being filled with a liquid ... peace. She looked into the face of her age-long persecutor. "You took everything from me," she said. "I didn't know what else to do. So I ran. But I'm not going to run anymore. And I'm not going to live as if I've already died because of you. You can't control me, or scare me, or manipulate me anymore.

It's just like the old man said: all things will be righted in the end."

The world changed color. Pinot looked around and saw that the earth was damp. A curl of the station's skeleton had kept her dry, and a puddle was forming where a drip fell in an endless ellipsis. For a moment, her past fell away from her and everything was fresh and quiet and new.

As she wiped her tears onto her palms, Pinot noticed something strange. The scars from her burns had marked her body to a disgusting degree, reminding her every moment of the horror and pain that she had endured the whole of her life. But as she studied the gleaming surface of her hand, understanding and a burst of crazy joy filled her. "Was I able to do this the whole time?" she asked herself.

There was a scuff on the gravel behind her. She turned to see Ed, his eyes pleading her not to run. She started to laugh, trying to show him her hand, what was inside her. She broke again, holding both her hands to her face. Ed placed a light, comforting arm around her shoulders, and if he could've spoken, she knew he would be saying over and over, "It's okay … it's okay … it's okay."

And for once, Pinot could believe that it was.

— ‹› —

May stood at the front window, anxiously chewing a hangnail and praying for them to appear on the horizon. "I shouldn't have been so angry with him in the first place," she scolded herself. It was a relief to be able to say things like that aloud, to feel like the words in her head were real and solid things that could cause waves in the air. Speaking had never seemed so important, but she reserved herself and went back to her fingernail.

Everything in the store was off, even the fluorescent hum of the lights overhead. Ed had never tried to control things remotely as far as she knew. He took his focus wherever he went, didn't brood on the past or Plato's forms like Isak did. May wondered if Isak had discovered what his gift was for. As they both agreed, their gifts had to be for something. The humming in her head, the tuning note of human presence in her life, was the lowest it had ever been. She was alone in the void of her thoughts.

And what did she find there but worry unending and material preoccupation? What had happened to her pictures of Van Gogh skies and philosophical forests? Her love of knowledge had become subservient to her need to survive. But hadn't she attained wisdom through what she experienced every day? Who said books or sages were the only paths to inspired thought?

She was interrupted by the swelling of a two-toned chord in her mind, a perfect fifth of caves and rapids. Pinot and Ed were returning. She looked out the front window, watching their approach. They walked side by side, Pinot explaining something with wild hand gestures. May realized that something was wrong with the picture: Pinot was smiling. "That's new," she said to herself. They had reached the gas pumps, when Pinot, half of her hair invisibly pale, pink tear marks down her cheeks, and a baggy sweater hanging over her like a robe, saw May and held up her hand.

"She looks like a saint," Isak said.

May nodded and blinked tears out of her eyes as Isak wrapped his arms around her stomach and rested his chin on her shoulder.

Chapter Four

The Partiers

May woke up screaming from the noise in her head.

"What? What is it? May, breathe, tell me what's going on."

"There's so many... Ah! It hurts. So much noise!"

Isak grasped what was happening and called out: "Ed! Ed!" There was no sound of reply. "He might be sleeping outside." Isak pulled on his clothes and went into the main room. May pressed her palms to her ears, hoping to block out the wall of sound building up against the door and the screeching crescendo passing into their sphere. She carried herself out of the room, not knowing what for, but not wanting to be alone.

The lights were on. Pinot was sitting stunned on the wooden bench. "What are they doing here?" she repeated to herself.

The bronze-clad creatures teemed outside the windows, around the gas pumps, their wide plastic eyes glowing white in the gray morning.

Isak ran up to Ed, who was sitting on the counter. "What are they?" he asked. Ed shrugged.

"Partiers." Pinot went up to the window, placing her forehead on the glass and cupping her hands around her face. Ed shook his head. He had never seen anything like this outside a video game before.

"I'll talk to them," May suggested, her eyes closed against the noise no one else could hear.

"You can't," Pinot said, pulling away from the window. "They don't speak English. I don't think they can tell a person apart from a lamppost."

"Why do you call them Partiers?"

"They stay in the city mostly, always travel in groups. It's like they carry around rave lights with them."

"They're intelligent." May nodded. "They just don't communicate the same way we do."

"Are you hearing all this, May?" Isak asked in a lowered voice. "Is it the frequencies?"

Ed raised his eyebrows at the back of Isak's head — *What are you talking about now?*

"I think so," May said. "I can... If I can get past the noise ... feel what they're feeling."

"And what's that?" Pinot asked.

May looked out at the mass of shells and glowing eyes, her gaze narrowing. "Anger."

"Then there's no way you're going out there to talk to them," Isak insisted. "If they're angry, they'll ignore reason. Who knows what they could do to you with those giant shell things."

Ed agreed by shaking his head — *Don't do it.*

May frowned and grabbed her jacket off the counter. "Maybe I can find out why they're angry."

"How?" Pinot asked. "I'm telling you, May, they don't speak English."

"Maybe not," May said. "But there's a human with them who might."

"What?"

"In the buzzing in my head, there are all these tones, and one of them is similar to yours, Pinot."

Isak placed a hand on her arm. "I'll go with you."

They swung open the door, letting it bang closed behind them. Ed and Pinot watched anxiously through the window as May approached one of the shelled creatures. A hatch opened and a young man dressed in neon and cutoffs with a chain of safety pins looped around his neck jumped down next to them. His hair was cut into a short, black mohawk, the front of which swept down over his forehead.

Pinot swore, but when Ed turned searching eyes to hers, she shrugged sharply and turned her focus intently on the unfolding drama.

It's like watching a cut scene, Ed thought. *I can't influence what's going to happen here at all.*

After a few words with the young man, May motioned him toward the store. He looked at her with a stunned expression, which turned grim as he stalked after her. Ed noticed the shudder run through Pinot's shoulders, but he pretended not to have seen.

Once inside, the young man leaned against the counter, facing May and Isak and Ed and Pinot with a self-assured and dangerous grin on his face. "I'm Jax," he said. He scanned each one of them, as if memorizing their forms for later reference. As he reached Pinot, his face faltered and flushed red with anger.

"Well, well, well," he growled. "There's the murderer's bitch. Where are you hiding him?"

"Shut your face, you Opaldine slice of vomit!"

"Pinot," Isak cautioned, fidgeting with the chain around his wrist.

"That's right," the young punk sneered. "The last one of all, Mills."

"My name is Pinot."

"You're one of his."

"Not anymore."

"That kind of thing is for life."

"He's dead anyway."

"What, you cut his throat? I know about that knife of yours."

Pinot grimaced, grasping the absent handle of a blade. "He died in an accident."

"He killed my gang. What was left of it, anyway. Unless you want to 'fess up? Unless it was you who stabbed Roch and Handel in the back and then ran off with our supplies? Huh?"

Pinot, fuming, made her way up to the counter. "So that's what this is? Some freakish revenge mission? How'd you get the Partiers on your side? Don't they have better things to do than follow a crazy flare like you around?" She threw an arm toward the window, revealing the infinity symbol tattooed on her wrist.

The punk folded his arms. "Be careful. Be very, very careful. That's all I'm going to say."

Ed motioned to Jax, finishing off a message.

"There's something he wants to tell you," May explained, when the punk remained planted in front of Pinot.

"He can bring it over. He's got legs, hasn't he?"

Jax snatched the paper as Ed came up to him, and scanned it. "So, you saw the body."

Ed nodded.

"Burned beyond recognition?"

He affirmed.

"Then it could've been anyone's." The punk crumpled the paper and dropped it onto the floor. "We'll search the place." He looked over the room, grinning sideways and scuffing up his mohawk. "Bye Mills. I'll be just outside if you need me."

Pinot glared at him, her hands clenched. Isak and May stood on either side of her with a hand on each shoulder. As the doorbell faded and the Partiers began to circle the store, May let out a breath.

"You're wrong about them, Pinot," she said. "The Partiers. They're all human."

Chapter Five

Isak

I can't sleep. *The Partiers are out there, completely still. Is May right about them? That there are humans inside those shells? They've suddenly become part of our weird landscape, blending in with the earth, wandering like tribes of old over the sterile tundra. Do they sleep, like we do? Maybe if I listen very closely — nothing. Just the sound of May breathing. She looks so tired when she sleeps, and her jaw keeps clenching. It must be the strain of all these people around, the static she calls it. If only we could— No! Stop thinking ahead. Thoughts like that, they'll carry you off into time — She's kicked off her blanket. There. Stay warm. You're so beautiful. I can feel your ribs, against mine, they're sticking out too — I must follow Seneca and desire nothing — There: the sound of my own breath, expiring in a moment, just as our lives before God. It's dark in here. I wonder if Ed can turn on lights in his sleep. His body is curled, like a question mark on the floor. He has such a gift, but losing his voice— Did we also have to make a trade? What did I lose in trade for this cursed ability? How much time have I lost? Was that question a desire? But I haven't moved. Does that mean there isn't a time when I know the answers or I've finally managed to separate myself from my thoughts? Pinot's sleeping pretty well on that shelf. Maybe it reminds her of home. She told me about her little sister; I wonder if they had bunkbeds? That's too close to curiosity — I have to be more careful! I'll just stare at the ceiling and not think... Did Pinot really* *kill them? Is her knife still safe?* — *Yes, it's there, the metal hilt, under which layer* — *the second flattened cardboard box from the floor. Who would've thought cardboard would be so comfortable? Everything's so still. Jax isn't going to leave without getting something out of it. I saw it in his face. I don't think I can*— *Well, can we trust anyone? Damn, I have to*— *God! Help me think of something else, or fall asleep. I can't make out the ceiling tiles, it's too dark, too murky. And that sensation*— *Oh no, think about something else, block it out, all that Gatorade before bed, you idiot! Don't think about it, don't think about it*—

Isak opened his eyes to an outside sky as his fingers fastened the front of his pants. He looked down at the hole at his feet and sighed.

"Hey!" a voice punctured the air.

"Even better," he mumbled. "At least you won't wet yourself when he kills you."

The punk kid, his neon green shirt glowing eerily in the ashen twilight, circled around so the shoveled-out dirt was between them. "How'd you get out here?"

"Tunnel. Under the stairs. Didn't you find that one?"

Jax flashed his wolf teeth, seeming to relax. "Doesn't matter. Not much you can do to us. And I really don't think you'd run out on your people."

"You're right." Isak noted the wire bands around both of Jax's upper arms. "Those have something to do with your insect shell?"

Jax nodded. "They hook into our Survival Units."

"They're pretty cool looking." Isak looked back toward the convenience store, a low black block ten feet behind him. "How old are you?"

"Old enough."

Isak nodded and tried to make out how many Partiers were outside the convenience store. Jax stood with his arms folded, watching him. "You're taking us with you, is that right?"

"Can't leave you here to die once we take all your supplies. That'd be inhumane." Jax readjusted the safety pin woven through the flesh of his ear.

"What about Pinot?"

"I haven't decided yet."

"Decided?"

"Yes. I'm kind of in charge here."

"Seems like a big job."

Jax bristled, but seemed to take the point. "It's only because—" Jax broke off and turned away from Isak, glaring out at the wasteland. "I'm the only one who has lived in both worlds. They're too afraid to spend more than five minutes outside their Survival Units."

"Where did they come from?"

Jax smiled. "You think I'm going to tell you everything? You're not some friendly father figure, not even close." The young man's face became grim. "He's dead anyway."

"Both your parents?"

Jax hesitated for a moment and then nodded.

"What happened?"

Jax's mouth pressed into a thin line. For a moment, Isak didn't think he would answer. Then, Jax released a breath and said, "Listen. My parents weren't bad people. They died in the Event, like so many others."

"My parents died too."

Jax studied Isak, like he had studied them all before, only this time he didn't smile. "You seem like a good person. Not like that infernal Miller-ite you hang out with."

Isak shrugged. "What does being good really mean? What makes you think your parents were good, for example. Was it what they did, was it how they treated people? Was it their legacy?" Isak swallowed his next breath, before he could go any further. *Did I cross a line?* he thought. *Maybe I've just killed us all.* He looked pointedly at Jax, waiting for some kind of reaction.

Jax stared straight ahead for a moment, his face blank. Then he cleared his throat, pulled at a strand hanging down from his Mohawk. "You want to know about my parents? They were both scientists. Developed the Survival Units years ago, part of some incentive project on creating sustainable conditions in unfriendly environments. Maybe a NASA thing, I don't remember. A lot of the people here were testing the equipment further north against extreme cold and limited ground cover. When the world disappeared, they headed back here to see if any of the scientists who had kept them safe had survived. Since then, they've been wanderers."

"They found you, though."

"I recognized them right away. It was like being in a dream. Like my parents had come back from the dead."

"Seems like they left a pretty good legacy behind them."

"Yeah," Jax said, narrowing his eyes at Isak. "And it seems like you got me to talk. Anything else you're dying to know?"

Is this a trick? Isak thought. *I guess one more question couldn't hurt.* "Survival Units, they're called, right? What about their language?"

"A voice scrambler. The Survival Unit translates. A defense precaution against outsiders."

"Your parents were very thorough."

"Yes."

Isak's legs ached. He kept himself distracted, counting the safety pins in Jax's ears. As long as he could get through this conversation and as long as Jax left before him, he could keep his traveling ability a secret. "So, what are you going to do now?"

"We'll keep heading west. We've come across a couple pockets of life since the city. Maybe if we could find... We'll find something. You'll see."

"So we *are* going with you."

"It would be best for all involved."

"And Pinot?"

"She'll come too. She's a Miller, but she hasn't killed anyone. Yet."

"We'll look out for her."

"You seem like good people. Good people interest me." And Jax smiled, his sharp eyeteeth gleaming.

―― ⟨⟩ ――

Pinot turned from the front window, taking her fists out from her pockets, but it was only Ed. "They're guarding us like we're enemies or something."

I thought you were, he wrote on a piece of receipt paper.

"I have no problem with the Partiers. I just don't get *him*."

Ed held a splayed hand on top of his head — *Jax*.

"Nobody's ever talked to the Partiers, ever. It's almost a rule." She turned back to the panorama of copper shells and eyes glowing dimly in the midnight air.

I have a hypothesis. Ed was beside her, grimly staring out the window. *Can I tell you?*

"Sure, whatever."

You should have died when the power station went down, but you didn't, right? And then you found out that your tears have healing properties, right? Okay. What if it's not just your tears?

"You think that my body was healing itself as it was burning?"

All the liquids in your body.

Pinot burst out laughing. "So ... spitting on someone would be doing them a favor?"

―― 《》 ――

There was a painting May had never had the chance to start. They had attended a night at the symphony, a selection of Vivaldi or something, and it began with the viola player. A soloist in an off-the-shoulder evening dress standing mournfully at the front of the stage, her instrument and bow held loosely in front of her. She had thick, powerful arms, and a broad braid of blonde hair woven with dewdrop jewels. As she began playing, May decided she was a good player but too technical, and it easily would've faded into her memory if not for the bouquet presented to her at the end of the concert. It was the most vividly pink collection of blossoms May had ever seen. They sang against the starry night blues in the satin dress, blushing under the heat of the stage lights, the soloist's shy, appreciative smile complementing the flair of the petals. The painting would be Impressionistic, May's favorite style, from slightly below to elevate the musician, the flowers exploding with color, the performer's skin glowing, her face asymmetrical and heavy, animated with honest pride and that shy smile.

She had intended to paint it the next day, when she and Isak would be at her mother's. During these visits, Isak would sit in the living room armchair and write poetry while May stretched canvases and sketched in the fireplace room below. The townhouse had been built with openness in mind, many of the floors only extending partway over the subsequent level, leaving a railed balcony to overlook the lower rooms. Sometimes Isak would call down for a word or May would fill the house with a vinyl of Rhapsody in Blue on the hi-fi system. Mom would return from looking after her neighbor's two-year-old and quietly settle into the library corner and read until they were finished. Mom had three moles on her chin, and crooked teeth. She tied her gray hair back with bare elastic bands so the ends were always staticky and torn, and she wore massive beat poet glasses with thick rims that gave her the look of some wide-eyed mystic. May wondered what she would've done next if the world hadn't come apart. She wanted to ask her mom why those glasses and why she always left the room when they watched *Casablanca* and who she had loved and how many times she had emptied the laundry and found secrets fallen out of pockets. If she kept them in a jar. If death hurt. Was it better her going that day and missing all the uncertainty of slow starvation? Had she found their dead child in heaven, can you recognize someone you've never met?

Just before realizing she was dreaming, May found herself atop one of the balcony railings, tipping over into a dark hole with stratified walls, the wind pushing strands of hair into her mouth, her clothes twisting around her. She fell deeper and deeper, until suddenly there was a green flash of trees and a rich forest canopy exhaling into a cool ocean breeze.

She barely had time to notice Isak was gone before he appeared, reclining back on his elbows, his legs intertwined with hers.

"I have to tell you something," he whispered. "They're taking us with them."

"Where?"

"Wherever they're going. West, he said."

"We knew we couldn't stay here forever. Will they let us take the truck, do you think?"

"I'm worried about what's going to happen to Pinot."

"She'll be fine. We'll all be fine."

"I don't know, May."

"Isak. You're forgetting something."

"What?"

"You're forgetting about Ed."

Chapter Six

Jax

Your parents were really something, Jax.

I guess you could say that, yeah.

Hey. Don't worry.

I'm worried, Keats. I'm so goddamn worried I can't sleep at night.

I'll be fine.

Warm enough?

The SU's got me at a comfortable thirty-seven degrees. Hard to breathe sometimes though. I get confused about where I am, and then I feel, I don't know, trapped, or claustrophobic.

The air out here's no good for you, Keats.

Oh, I don't want to leave the suit. It's keeping me alive.

Yeah.

How do you do it?

Hmm?

Live on the outside?

It's a big fuck you to the universe, isn't it. And ... when I'm in the suit, I'm alone, you know. Outside, I can see you all, lean against you when I get tired. Get my bearings.

Maybe I'd be more willing to try it, if I wasn't dying.

You're not dying.

I think I am. My vitals are all over the place. The SU tells me when they spike and flatten, spike and flatten. It's only slowing my body's degradation. Your parents were brilliant scientists, but they weren't gods.

Fucking right.

They'd talk about you, you know.

Not interested.

Jax. No need to defend yourself.

Who said I was?

It must be hard sometimes, being around the SUs all the time, living in one. You want nothing to do with your parents, and now here you are, carrying on their legacy.

I don't see it that way.

It's a strange coincidence.

Coincidences are how the world works. It's all random chance, but it doesn't mean anything. Do you think someone like me would be talking to someone like you in an ordered universe?

Maybe we're talking for a reason.

But then you'd be dying for a reason. I can't accept that, Keats. Screw fate. Screw it to the sticking place and then stick a knife in it.

Well, coincidence or not, it's always good to see you.

I'll check in on you tomorrow. If we're moving too far and you need a break, tell me so we can wait.

To be honest, I sleep the whole day. Auto-pilot's the greatest thing.

Night, Keats.

Goodnight, Jax.

Jax stalked off, hands deep in the pockets of the jean jacket Isak had given him; Jax's old Opaldine trench coat had worn to tatters months ago. The rough blue material was an awkward fit, since Isak was taller with broader shoulders, and there was a button missing, the second one down. But Jax didn't mind. The nights were cool out in the wasteland, and sometimes it rained. He had the SU to keep him dry, but most nights, he walked like this, weaving his way through the bronze domes with their dim eyes. Most of the SUs ran on minimal power during their night stops. Some of them were paranoid that the suits would break down faster if they didn't save as much power as possible. But the suits were self-sustaining; very few of them had shown any sign of wear.

Up ahead was the boxy shadow of May and Isak's truck. Jax felt a sick feeling rise in his throat. He thought of turning back, running a self-diagnostic, and passing out in his SU. But his feet kept on at a reluctant pace, drawing him closer and closer to her fort of empty crates and slabs of Gatorade set up in the flatbed. He meant to keep going, get past it, but something stopped him. She was asleep; he could hear her breathing.

"Fucking Miller, piece of shit," he grimaced. Then his legs gave way and he slid down the side of the truck.

He took a quick inventory, moving his toes around in his boots, listing his name and the names of his Opaldine initiates, all dead. He remembered everything. He could still move. But still he waited, not quite willing to risk another fall. What was wrong with his legs? Was the outside finally getting to him?

Above him, he could hear Pinot breathing in her sleep. Breath in, breath out. Instinctually, his breathing lined up with hers. In. Out. In. Out.

In went the knife. He imagined Miller cutting into Roch, who wouldn't hand over a bottle of wine. Out they ran, Miller dragging Pinot along, dissolving into the wilderness. Into the basement Jax went, just back from a scavenging run, to find all that was left of the Opaldine gang.

Yet, here they were, inches from each other, breathing in sync. It was too bizarre. How did they end up here, on the same patch of earth, on the same earth at all?

Jax spread out his fingers and pressed his palms flush against the ground. Slowly, his senses buzzing, he pushed himself up to standing.

Pinot was still asleep. He could see the shadow of her curled up body through the crate slats. So pitiful. Still, he found himself looking at her a moment too long.

He stopped by the pool. An upturned bowl of plastic two meters across. They used it to catch rainwater, and refill their SU life support tanks. His parents had designed the bowl to rest perfectly on top of any SU, for easy transport. They all took turns carrying it. Even May and Isak, bungee-corded over the cab of their truck. They were fucking lucky to have that polluting piece of garbage. The occasional gas pump that Ed was somehow able to fix, the odd shed with an old red jug of lawn mower fuel; somehow it was enough to keep them moving along, day after day.

Jax dunked his face into the pool and let the water settle around him. It was dark and cool, and it eased the throbbing in his head. His thoughts drifted. Pinot's half-scarred face and shock of white hair, her shoulders hunched up inside the baggy hoodie she wore. *I won't kill her,* he told himself. *It's a different world. Maybe here, coincidences mean something.*

He came up for air.

Chapter Seven

Farmer's Field

They were three weeks out from the convenience store when one of the Partiers died. He had been ill, but young, a twenty-four-year-old named Keats. A regular tragedy of a life just beginning.

Isak remembered twenty-four well. It was the year he and May had gotten married. Was that really ten years gone now? He rubbed his leg out of habit, though the pain had faded away. Pinot's spit had helped immensely. After Ed's hypothesis about her healing abilities was proven true, they had salved cuts, bruises, and May's scarred hands to wonderful effect. Unfortunately, there was one ailment affecting them all that Pinot could not heal: hunger. He who had, back in those just married days, been academically full around the face was now a gaunt set of skin and bones, tougher, less inclined to sit in thought. He saw all the people shifting around him searching for rest and he wanted to do something about it. But how could they complain? Jax, though young himself, was a determined leader. He would march them on through the worst, even at cost to himself.

Jax, now there was a puzzle. He was still undecided about them, at times welcoming their presence with a short word, at others, assigning them the worst of tasks: digging holes, cutting open cans of supplies with knives, scrubbing down the shells of Partiers with old rags until their hands were chapped. And still, they worried about Pinot. Was their plan working? Had Ed been able to turn the young punk's mind toward her, did he wonder after her more tenderly now than at their first acidic meeting? Pinot didn't know about their scheme, of course. May had thought it best. Ed, running around in Jax's circuitry just to keep Pinot safe? What a messed-up Romeo and Juliet this could turn out to be.

Isak watched as May helped a stocky man with gray flecked hair dig a hole just big enough for the boy's wasted body. The day before, they had come across part of a farmer's field, overrun and gone to seed in the absence of a caregiver. The sight of green alfalfa, intermingled with delicate orbs of seeds, thistles, and wildflowers, after so much desolation and emptiness, had given the mass of Partiers a sense of direction again. They didn't grumble over their wandering; now they talked about forests and edible plants. Some were studying stalks of alfalfa under those shells of theirs.

This is a touchy business, appeared in front of him, written on a roll of receipt paper. Ed held it in his right hand, scribbling something else. The canvas jacket, which he wore constantly, bagged over his stick thin arms. Stubble covered the lower part of his face and his eyes were wide and red.

"I think it's working, though. Just don't let him get too interested in her."

It's not mind control.

"You've explained that."

Ed breathed heavily through his nose, and wrote another line: *I can only turn his head in her direction, I can't make him look at her.*

"Keep trying." Isak's face changed into a softer look of concern. "You look tired."

Ed grinned, but couldn't maintain it; the inherent innocence in his face was slowly being chipped away. *How long before they bury the guy?*

"Shouldn't be too long," Isak said, rubbing the place where a chain disappeared below the frayed collar of his t-shirt. "Poor kid."

Ed tucked the receipt paper into one of the deep square pockets on his jacket, gave Isak a lazy salute, and wandered off until he was lost amongst the herd. "Poor kid," Isak said again, looking after him.

They buried the boy in the field next to a fence post that had an orange spray-painted mark down its center. Barbed wire flared from either side, cut off at both ends and left in the bored hole. To Isak and May, standing silently side by side, it looked like a thorny crucifix. Ed was called over to help take the boy's body out of its shell. The only Partier who had come out to carry the body was the man with salt and pepper hair. His lip quivered as he, Ed, and Jax lowered the corpse into the hole and began to cover him over with earth.

"Is anybody going to say anything?" May whispered.

Pinot came out of nowhere, scrambling through the shells of the Partiers, all turned inward out of respect. She stopped next to Ed, and looked over at Jax. His shoulders lifted slightly, and he nodded.

Pinot began, her voice carrying over the assembly, "Today, we're burying a young man, who survived an uncountable number of trials. He was one of you, Partiers, a strong and spirited member of your tribe. You lived together and grew together. You suffered loss together, because who of us hasn't lost someone?" She paused, seeming to see something in the distance. "Now, he's gone. He's left us, we hope, for someplace better, where he won't have to fear trouble in life, or fear the approach of death. His sickness has been taken away. Let's remember him always."

Who is this? Ed thought. Pinot's face, healed by her tears, though still discolored, looked ... vulnerable. She sat next to the grave, and stared at the ground. Ed had tears in his eyes. But that didn't stop him from noticing that Jax was staring at Pinot without any prompting from him at all.

Chapter Eight

Pinot

Go west, young man, and what will you see? A land without roads, wide open spaces yawning onto a flat line horizon. A copper plate under the vaporous sky. We hardly know the sun is there, diffused through so much fog. Sometimes it rains. Sometimes we come across an empty house or an apple tree. Our stomachs consume our awe at being alive.

Emptiness, though, makes it easier to be filled. I've looked everywhere for peace and only found sex-drugs-violence-broken glass-bruises-open handed strikes-the sound of metal tools hitting the floor. Now, sitting up here, looking out past the domed backs of our captors, out to that flatland and frowning horizon, I see past the thin skin of our reality. I see beauty, and the sweat of perseverance. I see that I am small. I see that the small are used to overthrow kingdoms. I see myself, with my legs hanging down, with my heels kicking the driver's side window, my halved face a grotesque puzzle set in thought. And suddenly, my thoughts return to earth. I pity myself; I feel a knot inside me that is untwistable.

The Opaldine is passing by, he glances up, and although I expect a retort, there is none.

"Hey, Slice!" I throw down. "What's the news on the street?"

He pretends not to hear, but I know better; his senses are Sherlockian. Something compels me to say ... that without him, we would all be dead. He walks on. I can see the dust streaking the back of his jean jacket, and I am too tired to clamber down after him...

May and Isak move through the Partiers like doctors, bending down to examine edges of shells and talk with them. Ed is asleep in the back of the truck. He's developed a tremor in his left hand and he feels cold all the time. "Ed?" I call back, spinning on my seat and lowering myself onto my stomach. From my vantage, he's small, curled on his side, covered in May and Isak's worn quilt. His hair is matted and his face is painful to look at, wasted and rough with stubble.

Isak gave me back my knife when we left Ed's place. He said I shouldn't need it anymore, but who knew what was out there? I swing around and slide off the cab, bare feet hitting our last case of Gatorade. Over and around bundles of books and extra clothes, the plastic basin we use to catch rainwater. Ed doesn't stir, doesn't hear my approach. I kneel down at his head, pull my knife, and take a clump of that greasy red mess in my hand. Gently, so he doesn't wake up, I start sawing off the matted chunks. His hair'll be short again. Maybe he'll feel better for it.

The pile stacks up, clumps of dead cells uncombed and tightly woven as moss. There's a dryness to his skin, his forehead. Even his nose looks exhausted. "When's the last time you ate something?" I ask, though I'm sure it's been days. There's not much left of our stash; the back of the truck is becoming empty like the wasteland, grooves of metal underfoot instead of sterile earth, but I'm sure I can find something. Putting away my knife, I saunter to the back corner where there is a petty pile of crates. Cans of water chestnuts and coconut, some beef jerky. A long metal handle.

"What's this?" I pull it free from behind the stack, swinging it overhead like a sword. There's a five-sided hole in the end. Some kind of wrench? "What is it?"

"It's illegal."

May's leaning her head on the side of the truck bed, her face gray.

"I was just looking for something for him. He hasn't, that's not—"

"No. *That's* illegal." She lifts her chin toward the long metal thing in my hand.

I hold it between us, so her face is framed in the pentagonal-shaped opening. "What is it for?"

"We would've died without it. I wonder how he knew."

"Who—?"

"'When you have kids,' he said, 'they'll need something like that, some bright deluge into the sky that will give 'em some awe of life.'" She readjusts herself, propping her arm under her head like a pillow. "We never had any. Kids. But we needed it anyway." She's somewhere else, her free hand working through her hair at her temple, a nostalgic smile settling around her tired eyes. "'Go cause some mischief...' We would've died without it."

I lower myself onto one of the empty food crates, resting my arm on the brim of the truck bed. "May, what is it for?"

"You never saw our house, did you? We had a fire hydrant on our front lawn. It was blue and yellow ... but Dad was a plumber, not a fireman. I always wondered how he got his hands on one of these. It gave us water. It gave us life." She holds out her hand and I place the bar there. We're connected by it for a moment. Then I let go and she tucks it down along the side of the wall. "Is everything all right?" she asks.

"Sometimes."

"How're things with Jax?"

"Why should they be any different?"

"Has he talked to you?"

"Besides insults and his sick Opaldine word vomit?"

"But nothing...?"

"What's Jax gotta do with me?"

"He hasn't killed you yet."

"I haven't killed him." May's eyes widen, like she's surprised at something. "What?"

"You don't entirely hate him."

"I despise the sterile earth he walks over."

"No," she says, moving closer and looking right through me. "No, you don't..."

"Is this your 'sense' thing again? You can't pretend you know what I'm thinking!"

As if agreeing, May breaks off and walks over to the back of the truck. "How's Ed?"

"Look for yourself." I follow above her, stopping next to him as she steps up onto the serrated metal end. She kneels down next to him.

"He's worse," she says, soft and kind of sad. "He shouldn't be pushing himself so much. Ed," she says, gently shaking his shoulder. "Take a break. Talk with us a while. Ed..."

His eyelids flicker and his mouth opens and closes, as if it's on a hinge. He exhales slowly, the escaping air sounding like a back-alley sigh. His left hand taps three times on the blanket spread out underneath him.

"Looks like Pinot did a number on your hair," May says, smiling at him in a bedside way. I can tell she's going to look at me next, and smile in the same way with some kind of direction in her eyes. But before that can happen, before Ed can sit up, I slip over the side and wander unnoticed through the Partiers.

Chapter Nine

Outside

The meteorite had traveled two thousand years across the empty black of space, that great vacuum of color, heat, sound, warmth. On the night it broke through the atmosphere of a formerly emerald earth, Ed was lying in the back of the truck, his lips chapped and bleeding, his brain nearly fried from electrical manipulation, his canvas coat open over his fevered ribs. When the meteorite burned through the dull gauze stretched over the sky, he was thinking, *Is there a point?* Everything fell around him in a chilling dew mist that tasted strangely of paprika, stinging his eyes. He lay there, uncertain of this place, thinking of Isak and May spending the night in the cab while Pinot slept in a room she had made with crates and boxes emptied of supplies. Were they awake, had they seen what he had? Could they explain what it meant? He tapped on the truck bed; no one answered.

His dreams were like static. They woke him up, back into the labyrinthine corridors of Jax's nervous system. The only mind he was allowed to explore. It exhausted him, all the signs of habit, the pruned off neurons, the vivid colors of the optic nerve, the pulses from the frontal lobe he couldn't quite decipher. Jax, functioning, unaware of the intruder clomping so unceremoniously through his mind. Unaware of an outside influence, maybe, but still able to reject Ed's suggestions.

Even though May insisted that Jax needed to be controlled at all times, Ed was finding himself with less and less to do.

Jax was seeking out Pinot on his own now; Ed was little more than an observer. Could he read thoughts, see Jax's dreams, file through his memories? No. All those doors were closed to him.

Pinot had become more reserved since the unexpected eulogy, but still surprised them all by smiling on occasion. At one of the patches they had come across, she had found a duffel bag of spray paint cans. Earlier today, Ed had suggested a pause to Jax, who was walking past the truck Pinot was busy covering with elaborate graffiti.

"Hey, Mills."

"Hey, Slice."

After a tense moment, Ed heard Pinot throw Jax a can, the ballast in the spray head clacking as it flew through the air. He saw Jax catch it. Without words, they covered the vehicle in slogans, elongated faces and starbursts, other things that didn't exist anymore. Ed lay in the back of the truck, listening to the hiss of escaping air carrying pigment and embedding it into the peeling side of the truck.

Now, lying in the truck bed, feeling the meteorite mist beading together and running down his face, Ed remembered how Pinot's acceptance of Jax had felt. It had hurt him, somehow, but he couldn't remember why... The day was arriving, clothed in elven gray, and even before fire burst through the horizon, Ed could feel the heat on his face. *What—?*

Pushing himself up and squinting past the side of the truck, he nearly choked on what he saw: a completely clear sky and the sun suspended over the horizon like a hot air balloon.

After being diffused through clouds and fog for so long, Ed had forgotten how bright it was, how searing and brilliant and bursting. He was close to being on his knees. But ... what would he be bowing to? A massive body of hydrogen? A chariot galloping from horizon to horizon? A lantern hung in the sky? It was life-nurturing flame that someday would go to ash. As he watched the sky warm and the glowing disc in his peripheral rise, Ed decided that he would never again venture into Jax's mind, for good or for ill. There had always been something unpleasant about it, even without Pinot ... and dear God, he was tired, worn, burned out, weary, exhausted, brain-dead, beat. He couldn't live this way anymore.

And neither, apparently, could the Partiers.

Jax, sleeping stretched out on the ground, heard a rustling all around him. And as he opened his eyes—

May, sitting in the truck cab with her eyes closed, so used to, by now, the hum of life around her that the sudden wave of feeling that was shivering through their camp had woken her up to discover that—

Isak, who had skipped the past three days, perhaps out of hunger, or desperation, May didn't know, suddenly appeared in the midst of the Partiers who were—

Pinot was on the roof, crying because—

Was it the dawn that drew them out, the sparkling new sky that looked like it did in paintings, in movies, in snapshots, streaks of mauve and peach blending upward into a pale baby blue? People were interspersed in the landscape of metallic mounds, glinting bronze in the sunlight, and all of them were silent. Such a sight hadn't been seen, of a fleshy crowd blinking and vulnerable, since the Event which had made them desert wanderers carried along in shells. Safety now had become second to awe. They breathed full, unfiltered air, their bare feet and hands communing with raw earth.

Ed was surprised to see a child sitting on one of their laps. It was the man with the black and silver hair who had helped carry the young man to his grave. A woman sat next to him, her dark hair and skin enhanced by the slanted beams of the rising sun. At the same time, they both raised a hand to the other, probably the first contact they had had in months. There were things that living in an SU didn't allow you.

For the first time, Ed counted the domes: there were twenty-five of them, a regular tribe, more like rounded houses now that their live-ins were out of doors. They wore simple, light shirts and shorts, silver-tinged white in color. Thin silver bands flared from their shoulders. Every one of them was sitting because most didn't have the energy to stand; their suits were set at minimal levels, providing enough nutrition and muscle stimuli to keep them alive and awake, but not spry or powerful. Jax moved among them, looking dazed and out of place in his grungy jean jacket and boots. Some gave him weak smiles as he passed, but no one attempted speech. They sat and watched the sun rise until noon, and even then, when there was no chance of it getting any higher, they remained. They were all remembering, Ed, May, Isak, and Pinot with them.

Dusk spread through the sky and, with a slow regularity, each person re-entered their SU, climbing down through the top hatch feet first, the thin solar sheets rustling as they reattached them from the inside.

"Did that really happen?" Pinot's voice came from the top of the cab.

Ed felt the same way, as if it had all been a vision they had somehow been able to share. The dimming plain gaped as lonely as it had been the day before, but he couldn't help but wonder if more changes were coming — and, if they did, would they feel any more real?

Chapter Ten

Green

Leaving the truck behind had been hard. It was the last piece of their past lives they had managed to hold onto, the last sense of a home base. Now they were on foot, dwarfed by the Partiers, with light packs on their backs and bare feet. Isak was starting to limp again. He had their quilt draped over his shoulders and looked like a homesteader with his tanned skin and dark, tangled hair. May had the wrench tied to the top of her backpack, which was filled with a couple of books and all the food they had managed to scavenge from the small abandoned patches they had run across. Pinot had the duffel bag slung across her back, holding extra clothes for them all and her paperback Salinger novel. Ed had his pockets packed full of receipt papers. All his writings from the convenience store were bundled in a plastic bag hanging from the rope tied across his chest like a sash. Their other supplies were also tied along this rope, so that Ed looked as though he had become entangled in a street vendor's display.

They never had to go far, just a few hours in the morning and a few at dusk. Jax never pushed them beyond reason; the goal was movement, not necessarily destination. Although Jax had told Pinot that what he really wanted was to see if the sea was still there.

That morning, after a restless sleep, Pinot had hoisted her bag over her shoulder and gone to the front of their camp where Jax was conferring with a couple of the Partiers.

"Mind if I walk with you today?" she asked Eliot, who she had recognized by a number printed above one of the insect-like eyes; each was a sensor set to absorb environmental information, air quality, UV rays, the like. Eliot, who had disabled her voice scrambler, answered in the affirmative. Most Partiers wouldn't have done that much. There were those who still had a fear of "outsiders" and kept their conversations cryptic. Even May and Isak couldn't coax them into speaking plainly.

They continued west, with Jax and Matthew, who was an expert in geography, acting as navigators.

"By tonight, we'll be past the Rockies," Eliot said, her voice sounding hollow through the communication system.

"We're going to climb the mountains in a day?" Pinot scoffed.

"We're in the middle of them right now."

"But," Pinot said, shooting a glance behind her, "it's completely flat."

"I know."

"How? You got a map in there or something?" She tapped the shell playfully.

"The GPS satellites don't always send us information. They're on the fritz. We thought it was because of the added atmospheric interference, but more likely — nobody's calibrated them in over a year. That's the thing about these suits, they need outside input. Their programs assume it."

Pinot pushed further ahead, glancing around her. All was flat and static. No lampposts out here. Just a lack. "Even the mountains." There was no surprise in her tone. Things had ceased to shock Pinot long ago. Even the morning Miller had woken her up in the basement of some crummy dead house with blood on his hands, she hadn't been shocked. When they had walked through the patches of dead city to a newly installed desert, she had laughed and smashed bottles. She watched her feet pass over the packed dirt beneath her. Maybe some of it had graced mountaintops once. She stopped suddenly.

"Is everything okay?" Eliot asked as she caught up to where Pinot stood with her hand loosely pointed at the horizon.

"Green," she mouthed.

"Jax!" Eliot called backward. "There's something here!"

"What? What is it?" Jax called as he ran toward them. Matthew caught up, looming behind Jax's shoulder.

"I don't know." Pinot shook her head. "But it's beautiful."

It was barely visible, stretched along the horizon, but something about it seemed vast, and it was so very, very green.

"It's a forest," Eliot said. Pinot imagined her standing outside of her SU in a long brown coat over a black blouse and slacks, nodding as she made her assessment. "Which makes me wonder" — pushing up her glasses here — "is this real?"

"This wasteland might not go on forever," Jax said, allowing a rare smile. "Let's keep going."

It wasn't until the next day that the rest of the Partiers began to notice that something was out of place. And then, it was as if Technicolor had been reinvented. Ferns and tiny forget-me-nots spread out before them, giving way to saplings, brush, moss covered rocks, leftover glacial passengers. The earth rolled under their feet into coulees and shoulders of land. It smelled of mulch and vegetable rot, damp, simple — alive.

"Looks like winter has finally broken," Isak said to May as they lagged behind to stare up into the branches of a massive cedar. Some of the Partiers had climbed out of their units and were walking bare in the surprise of nature, with their SUs, set to auto-pilot, following behind them like curious elephants. It became a full forest, and even — *Birds*, Ed sighed, trying to pick a warbler out of the foreboding grandfather of a pine tree.

"Where's Jax's SU?" Pinot asked, as it dawned on her that there was no bronze dome dogging at his heels.

"Didn't you know?" Eliot replied, still encased in her automaton insect with a hundred plastic eyes. "He left it with the boy who died. If someone else runs across the site, they'll be able to communicate with us."

"Wouldn't the dead guy's shell have done the same thing? Why'd Jax have to leave his?"

"I don't know. He didn't die. Maybe that's the only reason."

They turned back to the new green wonders, tinged a beautiful gold in the dusk, out into the open hands of the horizon where the azure clouds were graced with purple hues as the sun blazed to light another sky.

That night, as they continued through the thickening vegetation with sustained wonder, another miracle reached out to them in the form of candles in windows, flickering somewhere on the hillside above them.

"More people?" Isak said, stopping dead behind the wondering group of Partiers. "May, what do you—"

He disappeared. With a cry, May rushed through to the front of the group.

"Where are you going?" Jax yelled after her.

"He's waiting there for me, he's waiting, come on!"

— «» —

It was dark in the forest, familiar and strange trees flashing past her in rushing streamers of evergreen and shadow. Isak was waiting for her, where the light was; he had wondered who had lit the candles and wanted her by his side when they found it out, she was sure of it. The ground was steep under her; she felt if she stopped for a moment gravity would pull her backward and roll her down into the underbrush like a soccer ball. She had lost sight of the candles, but they couldn't be much farther now. A branch caught on her skirt and she paused to wrench it free. Spots swam across her eyes. Was it a trick of the light, or were the trees ahead lessening? She pushed through and found herself standing on a shelf extending out from the side of the hill. She looked back, out over the silhouetted treetops and could see, far off in the distance, where the tree line ended and the wasted plains began.

"There's so much of it..." she said, looking up into the sky. Stars, like curious animal eyes, blinked at her. It wasn't until she returned to earth and was about to leave that she saw the man seated not five steps away from her.

He was simply sitting there, with his palms upturned on his knees and the moonlight picking out the silver in his hair. Deep creases ran from the edges of his eyes, which were closed and still. His clothes read only as shadows; it was his face that held her there, standing on the open ridge in a supernatural patch of time.

"May," he said. "You have a beautiful name." His eyelids drew back to show deep brown irises intent on some distant point across the wasteland. "Where are you running to?"

"Is it your gift," she asked, "to discover names?"

"I have been given some knowledge, and with it comes much trial. One cannot be without the other. Some bury their gifts in hopes of avoiding suffering, but that is a course which leads to a greater destruction. The destruction of self."

May settled her back against a rock face peering out from the hillside. She looked with him in silence at the silhouetted forest and the dim glow of the Partiers at the base of the hill. "I don't know what it's for," she sighed. "If only I knew what it was for."

"I'm sure you'll learn, in time."

"Do you know who lit all the candles? That's where I'm going."

The man shook his head, but May thought she saw a flash of sadness go through his face. "You will see when you get there. More than you'll want to see, I'm afraid. But don't worry. It's better that way."

"Okay... I have to find Isak. Thank you," May said, not quite knowing what for. The man nodded and closed his eyes.

Chapter Eleven

House of Candles

May pounded on the cool metal surface of the black door, glancing her knuckles against the heavy wooden staff that ran up the length of it as a handle. "Please!" she yelled. "Be here, be really here!" Receiving no answer, she slowed herself down until she could hear the world over the sound of her heart, all the rich textures of an evening in the forest; the crescendo of wind shaking leaves on branches, the sporadic humming of insects, the creaking of a weakened tree limb. She shifted her focus to the building. Yes, there was definitely life in there. At least one human life. She could sense how uncertainty's cold fingers jabbed at their ribs.

"I'm looking for my husband!" she called into the door. It wasn't a lie. Isak had skipped to when she found out what was inside the house of candles, she was sure of it. "My name is May! Will you let me in?"

She reached up a hand and grasped the handle, pulling it open. "Hello?"

A form bearing a candle approached her. It was a middle-aged woman wearing a long green robe over a loose knitted sweater and black pants. Her feet were encased in moccasins so dark in color they could have been her skin.

"Welcome," said the woman. "Welcome to our refuge."

"Is Isak here?" she asked, peering around. The woman's candle had ruined her night vision.

"You know he isn't."

As her eyes adjusted to the dimly lit room, May could make out groups of tables and chairs, a long counter on the far wall, and a bay window lined with a dozen burning candles, a great open space that could seat one hundred at least.

"Come, sit with me and have something to eat." The woman placed her candle down so that the short ivory stub set in its engraved bronze dish threw light onto the surface of a square wooden table. Without another word, she left May in the circle of weak light, returning with a plate of mushrooms and bread and a tall glass of what looked like milk. The woman sat down and motioned for May to sit as well. May sank gratefully onto the padded wooded chair, staring at the plate of food in front of her. She picked up one of the mushrooms and bit it in half.

"Thank you."

"Now," said the woman with the candle, "tell me what you've done."

"What I've done? You make it sound all serious—"

"It's you yourself who've made it that way. There's something behind your words, like you're ashamed of something."

"Your gift," May said, reading a feeling of calm knowledge emanating from the woman. "It's like mine."

"Yes," she replied and folded her hands on the table in front of her. "The rest will be here soon. Who knows when we'll have a chance to talk like this again. Tell me. What is it?"

May took a breath, exhaling slowly. She knew exactly what this woman was talking about and, even stranger, completely trusted her.

"I'm messing with things I don't understand. I... It took me a while to realize that what I was hearing at the beginning were hints of other people's lives. I was somehow sensitive to their thoughts and their feelings. But it just came off as static because I wanted to ... believe we were alone. I didn't want to hope for anything beyond what we had. But our world kept growing, it had to, and I had to listen and really learn to hear and understand what other people were saying. Now, it's so clear. It's gotten to the point where I can influence people — not force them to do things, just change their minds maybe. I used this influence on Ed, so that he would be willing to use his abilities to manipulate Jax, but now... We should have trusted that things would work out without us trying to fix them. There were other ways we could have protected Pinot." May shifted uneasily on her seat. "And I'm afraid if we tell Jax... I don't know what he'll do."

"Does anyone else know about what Ed was doing to Jax?"

"Just the three of us: Ed, Isak, and I, that is."

The woman slowly turned the candle dish.

"Isak feels it too. We haven't even been able to talk to Pinot lately. We're just ... too ashamed."

"Then everything must be brought to light." The woman nodded. "Once you tell him—"

May gasped. A hunched figure of a man appeared at the woman's shoulder.

"Don't worry. This is my nephew, Ulway." The woman gently pulled him around into the light. The candle showed a young man with wide eyes and a good-natured smile, a curl of dark hair circling over his forehead.

"How many of you are there?"

"People come and go. On the other side of the building" — the woman motioned to the back wall with a half-curled hand — "is a main highway. Travelers follow it here."

There was a renewed pounding on the door before it was violently wrenched open. Jax stopped at the sight of them, his eyes flashing in the candlelight, Pinot and Ed bursting in after him.

"Welcome," said the woman, standing with her hands spread on the table. "Don't be afraid."

"Do you know her?" Pinot asked, walking toward May with her old, careless swagger. "Jax thought you might be in trouble."

Jax jerked forward but, mid-lunge, seemed to change his mind and lowered himself into a chair instead.

"Ed, stop it!" May hissed, but Ed, with his starved eyes, shook his head.

"Who are you?" Jax growled. "What is this place?"

"It's a restaurant," the woman said simply, relaxing back into her chair. "My sister and brother-in-law owned it. They built it up from the hillside. Their whole lives were dedicated to every small food request or fixing up the leaky parts in the roof of the place. They hadn't been away for nearly fifteen years. So, I convinced them to take a holiday, just for a couple weeks. Ulway and I could take care of things. And we did, for a while. We thought when the power cut off and the Internet failed to connect that there had been a surge somewhere or a tree knocked over the lines — those things had happened before. But Carey and Malcom didn't come back. Traffic on the highway completely disappeared. The occasional traveler brought strange stories of how, if you followed the highway too far east or west, everything just disappeared. Ulway and I, after that, just tried to keep the place going, to help people however we could."

"And who are you?"

"Arissa."

Isak appeared with his hands behind his bent back and his quilt draped over his shoulders, staring intently at Arissa's face.

"May," Arissa said, with amusement tingeing her voice, "I think I found your husband."

Chapter Twelve

Disclosure

"And what an interesting man." Arissa's dark eyes ran over his face. "He has poetry written all over him."

Isak straightened up, his brows linking in perplexity.

Arissa noticed and winked. "I'm sorry if what I say doesn't always make sense. Sometimes when I look at people I can't help it." She put a hand on Ulway's shoulder, which May noticed was hitched up and bulky. "Can you bring over a couple more candles, dear?"

Ulway melted back into the heart of the room, reappearing as an outline dimly discernible in front of the bay window. He bent down and returned, a candle in each hand illuminating his face.

"You are welcome to stay as long as you like," Arissa said, turning her attention to Jax.

He shrugged in reply. "There are twenty-five more of us. We could use some supplies." Despite his usual arrogant ease, it was obvious to May that something about Arissa was getting under his skin.

"Where are you going?" she asked him.

"To the ocean. I want to see if it's still there." Jax cast his eyes to the side and bared his teeth, as if angry at himself for revealing that much to a complete stranger.

"Jax," she continued, "what is your ability?"

His breathing came deeper, his hands gripping the frayed edges of his jean jacket. To May, he felt like a spark about to catch on a pile of tinder. "I don't have one," he answered, grinding his teeth. "Not like the others."

Arissa rose slowly and cut a slice of bread from the loaf Ulway had placed in the middle of the table. "I think you do. There just hasn't been opportunity for you to use it. That's why you must continue west, because part of you knows where to find it." She took the piece of bread and placed it in front of him. "We will supply you with what you need for your journey."

Jax stared at the offering, before nodding sharply and ripping it into bite-sized pieces that he chewed with resolute intensity.

"And what about you?" Arissa returned to her seat and faced Ed, who was standing on the edge of the light patch the candles cast around the tables. He looked hunted for a moment, then crossed to her, sitting at the table and scribbling over two sheets of receipt paper. Arissa quietly read through the first paper and nodded, saying, "It's the best thing you can do now." Ed looked Arissa in the eyes, and it seemed to May as if the overhead lights flashed on and off again — but it had happened too quickly to know if it was real.

She noticed that one of the papers had appeared in front of her. Ed had taken one of the candles and was leading Jax to a table at the opposite side of the room. May held the thin sheet between her and the candle flame so the words were illuminated from behind: *I have to tell him.* She suppressed the guilty impulse to rush after them and rip up what Ed was undoubtedly writing down.

Pinot sat cross-legged on the floorboards. "How about me?" she asked Arissa.

The woman turned in her chair and sighed. "You are caught between two versions of yourself. There's a lot more, but maybe I shouldn't say, hmm?"

"Just say it to me."

Arissa leaned down, and whispered into Pinot's ear.

Surprise loosened the young girl's face before she bowed it into shadow. "Thanks," she said after a moment, lifting a calm smile to the candlelight. "I wanted you to be right."

"Don't be afraid," Arissa said, placing a hand on her shoulder.

Suddenly, Jax threw back his chair and came toward Pinot with murder bleeding from his eyes. "Damn it, Miller!" he said, stopping short in front of her, his chest heaving. "You're no different from the rest of any of them!"

Pinot rose to meet him, one of her hands lifting. "What the hell do you mean?"

"This is my fault," May said, trying to keep her voice calm. "Pinot doesn't know what you're talking about."

"I was wrong then." Jax bared his teeth. "You're not good people. You're twisted. You're sick. I commend your noble intentions," he spat toward Isak, "but you had no right to mess with — to mess with my head like that!"

Arissa rose in the middle of the tension like a flag of peace. "Pinot," she said, placing an arm around her shoulders, "is innocent. Don't let someone else's mistakes fall on her shoulders."

Jax narrowed his eyes, and turned toward the door. "I'm leaving," he said. "I'm taking the Partiers with me. Stay here. I can't... I don't want to look at your sick faces anymore." He shuddered, as if rejecting an impulse to turn back for one final look, and left through the heavy black door.

The force of its closing blew out the candles.

"Ulway," Arissa's voice came through the darkness, "some light, please."

The flare of a match revealed Isak, pale and sitting in a chair with his leg stretched out in front of him. May was standing next to the bread table, her hands clasped in front of her and her eyes focused on the dark window as if following Jax out into the forested night. Pinot and Arissa stood next to each other, grim, with shining eyes. May was first to notice that Ed hadn't moved from where he had told Jax their terrible secret.

"He's hurt," she exclaimed, rushing over to him. Ulway, holding a candle aloft, illuminated a grisly scene, of Ed with his head on the table and blood running across his face.

"Can you hear me?" May said, crouching down next to him. He moaned. "This was my fault. I'm sorry I made you do it. Why did you tell him, Ed? Why didn't you wait? I could've helped." She tapped the table next to his ear, gently: five-four.

Pinot lost no time. She held her hands to her still wet cheeks and then slowly started to wipe them across his face. She found the wound, a deep gash across the right temple, and spit in it. Arissa and Ulway appeared behind them with a bowl of water and washcloths. "Not yet," Isak said, his eyes watching Pinot and Ed and the pool of blood. It was obvious that Pinot wasn't the only one who carried a knife in her pocket.

She spit into the wound again, using her fingers to slowly massage it into his skin, her rose-cast ring gleaming softly. Holding her hand over the wound, she closed her eyes, and it seemed to May as if her lips were moving.

About the Author:

Brittni Brinn was born Brittni Ann Carey in Winnipeg, Manitoba. She studied English and Drama at Concordia University College of Alberta (now Concordia University of Edmonton) before moving to Windsor, Ontario for graduate studies. She received her M.A. of Creative Writing in 2015. She co-hosts Hardcover: A Literary Podcast and writes plays for Paper-Knife Theatre. Besides books, her interests include coffee, songwriting, and cyborgs.

If you enjoyed this read

Please leave a review on Amazon, Facebook, Good Reads or Instagram.

It takes less than five minutes and it really does make a difference.

If you're not sure how to leave a review on Amazon:

1. Go to amazon.com.
2. Type in The Patch Project by Brittni Brinn and when you see it, click on it.
3. Scroll down to Customer Reviews. Nearby you'll see a box labeled Write a Review. Click it.
4. Now, if you've never written a review before on Amazon, they might ask you to create a name for yourself.
5. Reviews can be as simple as, "Loved the book! Can't wait for the Next!" (Please don't give the story away.)

And that's it!

Brian Hades, publisher

Need something new to read?
If you liked The Patch Project, you should also consider these other EDGE-Lite titles:
——<>——

Shadow Life

by Jason Mather

He's back from the dead... and he's not the only one.

The city-state of Denver is tightly controlled. High-tech methods of food manufacturing and firm restrictions on reproduction keep the population stable. But even here, in this regimented society, violence is never too far away...

It was supposed to be a simple job. At least, that's what Hans Ricker was expecting when he agreed to deliver a mysterious package for five-hundred dollars.

He was not expecting to get torn limb from limb while making the handoff. Nor was he expecting to emerge from a coma fourteen months later in the mile-high Denver General Hospital, his original organs replaced with regrown tissue. And he definitely wasn't expecting to find himself entangled in a police investigation – one which takes a dangerous turn when an armed man tries to assassinate Greta "Grit" Ricker, Hans' estranged sister and head of Denver's security forces.

Shadow Life follows Hans Ricker as he sets out to find the person responsible for the multiple attempts on his and his sister's lives. Pairing up with "Onyx," a powerful Denver crime lord, Hans hunts down leads across the Midwest. From the overpopulated religious commune of Salt Lake to the mountains of Colorado, Hans and Onyx fight for their lives against drones and lab-grown human constructs, gradually unraveling the mystery of who wants them dead, and why...

Shadow Life is a high-octane adventure set in a deeply layered near-future world of complex political arrangements and fascinating new technologies, a must for fans of science fiction and cyberpunk.

Praise for Shadow Life

"Jason Mather's "Shadow Life" (Edge-Lite) blends the societal intrusiveness of George Orwell's "1984" with a sci-fi adventure of George Lucas in a timely manner."
— Jeffrey Hatcher

"This is an incredibly readable book. From the first line, I was taken in and absorbed by the story, which has just enough science fiction in it to be intriguing, but not so much that you feel bogged down by the technical details."
— sbinwa, amazon

"An excellent book. Rich characters. Great pacing. A page turner from start to finish."
— Zennifer

For more on Shadow Life:

tinyurl.com/edge6030

—— <> ——

Tooth and Talon

by Alex Hernandez

Humanity and creatures on an exoplanet are bound by tragedy.

Humanity tamed the solar system and their bodies using powerful nanomachines. Now, Oya Valette and a group of colonists are looking for a fresh start on an extrasolar planet. Soon they discover that their new home is already populated by hostile, extravagant creatures that share a tragic history, not only with the human race, but Oya herself. If Oya can't set aside her own prejudices and reconcile these two warring factions, both will become extinct.

"Tooth and Talon combines all of the ostentatious elements I loved about science fiction, interstellar colonization, cyborgs, genetic engineering, robots, dinosaurs but they're used in the service of an immigration story. It's ultimately a story about starting over in a new land full of opportunity and peril. It's about the cost of assimilation and it's deeply informed by my own family's immigrant experience."
— Alex Hernandez

Praise for Tooth and Talon

"With his new novel Tooth and Talon, Alex Hernandez fulfills the promise of science fiction to envision new worlds, fantastic future worlds, and then through the force

of its characters, convince you that this future is just on the horizon. The novel imagines how genetic engineering and nanotechnology can transform human society, providing us with wings and powerful life-extending nanobots. It holds these human modifications in the balance, and while they do not erase the human condition, they certainly make life more interesting! Tooth and Talon is a wonderful addition to the growing corpus of Latin@ science fiction. Firmly grounded in the Caribbean experience, the novel delves deep into our quest to retain our humanity amidst technology that threatens to overwhelm us."
— Matthew David Goodwin, Editor of Latin@ Rising: An Anthology of Latin@ Science Fiction and Fantasy.

"I loved this book! The story hooked me right away with the intense prologue. The idea of a genetically modified species clashing with humanity was done really well."

"The characters were interesting, and the main character's cultural background was something I hadn't read before and was fascinating. There were also some great connections between characters from the past to characters in the present."
— MMB

For more on Tooth and Talon:

tinyurl.com/edge6027

——— <> ———

Yesterday's Savior

by Keith Bliss

A crisis of faith!

By the year 2075 most of the western world has converted to the religion of the Church of the Second Coming. From its humble beginnings, as the figure of Christ began to appear all around the globe, the Church has grown to achieve absolute world power. But rumors surround the Church of the Second Coming, and hint, like so many regimes before it, of deeply held secrets and the use of brutal power to quiet 'those who oppose.'

When David Dyson, a devout priest working for the Church, and a true believer of the Second Coming, is interviewed by a tough female reporter about the outrageous rumors surrounding the Church, Dyson discovers that his whole life may have been built around a lie.

Will his crisis of faith reveal the Church of the Second Coming's astonishing secrets? You'll be surprised by the revelation and shocked by the misunderstanding of the brutal regime.

Yesterday's Savior is a reminder, particularly relevant in this day and age, that freedom is worth fighting for.

Praise for *Yesterday's Savior*

"What do you do when the basis of your entire career preparation and personal belief is suddenly proved wrong. Father David Dyson, the main character, struggles with this dilemma. Is it right to tell the world that they are worshiping under a false pretense even though that belief has led to world peace, or should Dyson silently go on with his life, keeping that knowledge to himself?"

"Yesterday's Savior by Keith Bliss, is a mystery novel that took me on a quest for a truth that was initially hinted in an historical sheet of paper. How will Father Dyson gather convincing proof to make others believe. The church built on this false premise controls the police, the politicians, and wields a secret police unit of its own that it uses to effectively quash dissent and truth. The whole world is now united under one religion and crime is almost non-existent. How can this church be a bad thing? Father Dyson must decide that for himself if he is to move forward in bringing the church down."

— R. Ploude

"Yesterday's Savior is a good read for anyone who enjoys the mystery involved in conspiracy theories. Author Keith Bliss wrote of a world wide religion based on an event in 2010 and how by exploiting people's faith "the church" is much more than a place to worship on Sundays!"

— Christa

For more on Yesterday's Savior:

tinyurl.com/edge6026

—— <> ——

For more EDGE titles and information about upcoming speculative fiction please visit us at:

www.edgewebsite.com

Don't forget to sign-up for our Special Offers

Made in the USA
Middletown, DE
31 March 2018